# CONTENTS

| | |
|---|---|
| Foreword | 1 |
| Introduction | 2 |
| The Last High Tide in Salisbury | 9 |
| Mission Paradoxical | 21 |
| Paradox Lost | 23 |
| Decorating | 43 |
| Married at First Sight | 45 |
| Zenith | 54 |
| Sebastian | 58 |
| The Walker | 59 |
| The Forgotten | 60 |
| The Away Match | 69 |
| The Crossing | 78 |
| The Hairdresser | 79 |
| The Coalmine | 82 |
| Freda – The Interview | 89 |
| Olaf's Big Adventure | 92 |
| April Shower | 102 |
| Stonehenge Scaffolding | 114 |
| Empty Room | 120 |
| Scales | 122 |

| | |
|---|---|
| The Colonists | 123 |
| Dolphins | 128 |
| Screen Time | 132 |
| The Hunter | 134 |
| Rust | 136 |
| Season Ticket | 140 |
| Jemimah's Choice | 142 |
| About The Author | 158 |

# Foreword

The object of reading is often to see the world from a different point of view. Sometimes just to see inside someone else's head. Think how strange the world seems in the past. Now imagine what it would be like for someone in the future looking at us. The introduction tries to overcome this disconnect from a future which has more in common with our past.

# Introduction

This collection is mostly a result of the reclamation initiative. If you work dismantling redundant buildings you will know that you have been asked to send any writings you find to the National Archive. Some of these stories require understanding what the world was like in the past. I have added a few explanations in this introduction to assist.

These stories are mostly about people and relationships. These things do not change but circumstances and context do. Most of these stories were written almost two hundred years ago which seems to have been a more interesting time. I spent some of my volunteering at the National Archive. I continue to go there at least once a year because the volunteers there always have something interesting to tell me. I must thank them all not only because they alerted me to the ones that they found interesting, but also their enthusiastic research brought the stories to life.

We all know that since that time much that was commonplace has disappeared, we have a protective amnesia which allows us to enjoy life. The National Archive affords the comfort that unlike previous civilisations we have not actually forgotten. Very few enquire within because it could be upsetting to really understand what has gone. Technologies are the most obvious loss but, maybe because not everything was perfect there was escapism. Stories about fantastical things which sometimes became reality. Would they have happened without the vision of the writer?

Having talked about the past the first story is set in a future. **The Last High Tide in Salisbury** is a scenario that could have occurred if the world had carried on as it had for the previous century. Back then the climate was changing; the worst effects were stopped by the calamity and we are living in a better world than may have been the case. This story was probably written as a warning. There were many scientific studies and projections but none of them felt real. Before you judge the choices of the characters imagine yourself in their place.

Travelling in time was a popular background to many tales; it is the ultimate escape from the present. Many stories revolved around the temporal paradox - someone from the future affecting the past. How can you be sure that you are not going to change the future such that you would not be there to go back to cause the effect? Pondering that question you can enjoy **Mission Paradoxical**.

I hope you are wondering what happened next. **Paradox Lost** explores some of the difficulties faced by time travellers. It seems that you must lose your free will once you are in the past. You can only enjoy life when you do not know what is around the corner.

One form of time travel we can all indulge in is **Decorating**. Often we simply add another layer creating a timeline to be discovered when there is a renovation. Sometimes in the 'untouched' cupboard or under an old carpet there are better preserved echoes of the past. Very occasionally there is a story which is completely up to date. This story is two intertwined timelines.

To understand **Married At First Sight** you need to know that marriage was a contract between two; usually a man and a woman; there were as many men as women back then. It was a union not only of two people but also their property. This was important because there was the concept that everything was owned by someone. This included places to live so it was possible to be homeless. At this time most people had a handheld device which allowed them to talk and send messages to anyone who also had a device. Stranger still you could allow someone to know where you are as a moving blob on a map.

My mother found love when I was still young. The object

of her affection had travelled and she told me of the exotic places she had seen on the way. **Zenith** is from the millennium before last. There is a lesson for us all - that civilisations rise and fall. Some recorded their existence in detailed stone carvings and that is how we know of them. If you travel far enough south you will find that the sun is overhead, at zenith, twice each year either side of the solstice. It is, therefore, no surprise that one may worship the sun and accord these times special meaning. Can you imagine a world without the wheel and vehicles to help you move things around. A society just a few days walk away could be very different from your own. The characters in 'Zenith' have this same disconnect.

One character in Zenith has two personas. **Sebastian** has an alter ego but it sits well within him. **The Walker** just has one at a time.

Two hundred years ago a man set foot on the moon. Fifty years later people were talking about living on the moon and maybe going further. Experiments were conducted to see how a society might develop if cut off from the world for a generation. What would it be like to live in a closed group where every job was important; population was strictly controlled and there was a limited choice of partners. **Forgotten** explores this.

The Shard is one of the wonders of London. The large wind turbine at the top and hundreds of smaller ones provide much needed electricity. The elevation and storage of water are even more important for a small constant supply. Its utility is forgotten because of the wonderful cascade when the reservoirs are full and the wind is blowing. It is a long climb up the stairs to the top but the view is worth it. A long time ago before it was reclaimed The Shard was a dwelling. Those who lived there had lifts to save them the effort. I have calculated that to own a home in the upper reaches would cost more than a normal person could earn in lifetime. To achieve that status you needed something special; obviously luck helped but an understanding of how the world worked was also useful. **The Away Match** is when an ordinary man meets an extraordinary woman and generates some luck but unfortunately not for himself.

**The Crossing** is unimaginable now. In the past people moved around so much more and so much more quickly. Even though there were many more people there were still not enough for every job. Automation was the solution. I do not want my explanation to be longer than the story itself, you can console yourself that the combination of circumstances could never happen now.

My hair is part of me, my sense of myself; only friends touch it. My mother used to brush my hair when she wanted to tell me something. When she fell in love she said nothing but every strand was separated; only lovers caress it. I look after it myself with help from special friends. The concept of styling it seems slightly alien but in the past **The Hairdresser** had this job; it was still intimate but in a different way. You treated your hairdresser as an extension of yourself; sharing thoughts, joys and sadness. I will only say that in a world dominated by men, women needed special skills.

The last years of our education are when we 'volunteer' to experience work and life in the adult world before making our choices. **The Coalmine** is an almost true story. I was asked to write a radio play which showed how working in a coalmine could be fulfilling. I went underground for just one day as part of my research. You cannot really work in that environment unless you have volunteered in the original sense of the word. I have included this story not to create more coalminers but to encourage a few of you to become writers.

Next is a completely true story. I was only a girl when I interviewed those around me for 'The Chronicles of Mollisham'. **Freda – The Interview** has references to that book but you do not need to have read it. I wrote this story for a special occasion.

Did you know that it will soon be two hundred years since the town car was invented? When there was more electricity than now you did not have to have enough to get home before you set off. **Olaf's Big Adventure** is the story of how just such a car created a friendship between two women even when it got off to a bad start.

The weather has changed in the last one hundred years. Luckily we do still have weather and the forecast is important. In the days of television the weather forecaster was regarded as a close friend. When the rain falls in Spring we call it a 'deluge'; back then it was still short in duration but slightly gentler; it was called an **April Shower**. This is the title of the story about a weather forecaster who became a different kind of deluge herself.

In this story there is a word which means something incomprehensible now. About two hundred years ago the Dark Ages began. In the National Archive it is the start of the period when everything was stored electronically. Back then you could ask a question and get answers which would take you years to find by reading. I found one reference to this in a story but I think it was a misprint. Because this possibility is mind-boggling the action of asking is called 'goggling'.

In the past when a group of people (usually men) did a job they formed a company. They had to give it a name. Where I come from 'Stonehenge' was responsible adjectivally for many trades. When Stonehenge was built they may conceivably have had 'plumbing' but 'printing' was not invented for four thousand years. In the archives there are references to **Stonehenge Scaffolding**. This story makes you wonder – they must have needed some to construct it.

How do you observe when your eyesight is failing? **Empty Room** considers how you may experience more using your other senses. I found some bathroom scales which were so old they used a different measuring system. **Scales** imagines what it would be like to have known this item all your life.

When there were more people some of them were free to do things which were not directly useful. They could study the natural world and what they discovered is in the National Archive. You need some idle time just to be able read what they found out. The octopus is an amazing creature, capable and intelligent; you would not eat them if you had read what I have.

To really put you off having them for dinner you should read **The Colonists**. By now you will have a feeling of how strange the world used to be. To other intelligent beings maybe our world is just as incomprehensible.

Another intelligent sea creature is the dolphin. Nowadays they are plentiful and can easily be seen from certain cliffs. Once they were much rarer and you would need to go on a special boat trip to see them. What did the dolphins think of this? **Dolphins** is a story told partly from their point of view. There was one special place where they thrived. Fishing had been banned around some islands where a President had chosen to have his private residence. A President was a combination of Queen and National Coordinator which is a ridiculous idea. One job is for life and the other just a few years so problems arose if a President insisted on the longevity of a Queen. For the dolphins, however, this was serendipity

I remember being frightened by the drain monster who eats the items flushed away by mistake. It was all so logical, if something goes down but not through it will cause a blockage. When the blockage was alive that was terrifying. Such a story is designed to frighten the reader, usually to show the consequences if they choose a particular path. **Screen Time** is a cautionary tale set during the Dark Ages when screens could hold the attention of anyone.

I understood **The Hunter** as soon as I read it. I may have more flights of fancy than most people or maybe I just like to write them down. I was visiting the caves with the stalactites and stalagmites. I am impressed by the imagination of those who display them with subtle lighting. On one visit the electricity failed and there was a brief, scary, period of darkness before some emergency green lights came on. That is all I need to say.

Have you ever wondered what it may be like to be an atom? If so, which would you like to be? Do they have different characteristics? Next time you do an experiment at school or have a drink or step on something – just wonder how they feel.

**Rust** will give you some ideas.

We live in a time where there is a diversity of accent and dialect in our language. In Mid-Pennine the word 'the' does not exist, represented here as t' but it sounds more like you are saying it backwards, sometimes a t added to the previous word. The letter 'h' is largely superfluous. In writing often these differences are absent, **Season Ticket** is about the ups and downs of supporting a football club. A translated version would not convey the intended meaning.

We all know how the story of Jemimah Bond ends. The jungle facility of the evil master criminal has been destroyed and she is awaiting rescue with the people she has saved. It was escapist because it denied the reality of the time, pretending that calamity had been averted. **Jemimah's Choice** is a different ending, the one which actually happened and we are living in.

History is written by the winners which is why what she decided seems natural to us. If you had been alive at that time you would probably have a completely different view. This story has references to many things which no longer exist I hope it encourages you to research the period to see what we have lost.

## The Last High Tide In Salisbury

They are all worth something. They hoped never to be here. Their number alone convinces them of their desperation. We all heard the message on the radio. Tomorrow the boats will arrive. The snow has chased them here; how can something so gentle have an iron grip. The cathedral alone seems defiant; not letting those delicate shapes settle on its spire.

They have exhausted their supplies so Tom has organised a hunting party. Snow does not take sides; the deer cannot hide. I collect those willing to forage. The summer has been kind to us; the hedgerows full of blackberries; an old orchard laden with apples for its final performance. Our son, William, is so happy; children cannot survive on adults alone.

My grandmother told me how the water got higher all her life; crowding the people. She was just a girl when the Fordingbridge Wall was abandoned. The town itself was already disappearing under the lake which was forming behind it. Its level was determined by the height of the lowest tide. Of course, collective disbelief at the speed of change meant the wall had been built ever higher. We are no match for fierce nature and when it failed it was pushed aside, disdainfully. A torrent of salt water rushed up the valley, licking the water meadows when it came to rest.

Her generation still believed they were in control. They dug the navigation channel and Salisbury became the port through which everything flowed. As the water came in everything else went out. How many tens of thousands have passed this way since the darkness made life precarious. Starvation is deadly but hunger is a driving force. Generations ago we were not so welcoming when the world was burning. Now we are beginning to freeze they have been more practical.

In return for anything which can be reclaimed they have provided food. In return for passage south you can mortgage your life. They know there are very few left on our islands so they broadcast the message; it was the last chance to leave and none would be refused. It has been five years since the last exodus boats. We have been subsisting but when the land is almost empty of people there is plenty to go around.

It is almost a feast. Conversation is focussed on the morrow. This is not a free ride. They are under no illusion as to their future. Alliances are made. It is far better to be a family unit; their new owners will tend to respect such things. I congratulate Tom on the success of the hunt. He points to a girl who seems alone. 'She is better than I ever was at that age. A strong, steady arm and a keen eye. She is responsible for the humane dispatch when others had sent them into a frenzy.' This is praise indeed from him to an equal.

'She seems unattached,' I observe.

'Her mother is negotiating, trying to find a man who doesn't see her just as an asset.'

'So what else do you know about her?' I ask this because I could see he had been affected by her. He is an open book to me, I still remember such things before they were all used to keep warm. When he was younger than this girl is now he had stayed to look after his grandfather, who would have been refused passage on a small boat. I stayed out of fear; I was a prize asset. When his grandfather died I comforted him and William was the result. This made me refusable so he stayed again.

'She has a younger sister, the one playing with William.' He points to the happiest people here. The sight of them makes me start to think about the future. I go over and ask the young girl.

'Where is your mum?' She points to a woman about my age; she is just leaving an argument and is heading our way. I do not have a plan but I offer respite from the stress of deciding between the lesser of two evils. 'You don't like men, do you?'

I say this as she bends to pick up her daughter. Her stoop turns into sitting on the floor. 'There is nothing to like about this lot.' This is muffled as her head is now down between her knees to the hide the tears which fail to materialise.

'Tom told me about your problem.'

She looks up at me, 'how can I protect her? She doesn't even want to go.' I look across at her elder daughter. I suddenly realise she is wearing animal skins that she has probably assembled herself. Then I notice that Tom is wearing the same that I have made for him. He seems fixated on her. Strange ideas are surfacing, am I replaceable? I look at the woman. She must be strong to resist the offers of these men. In fact to have two children and no partner she may have an aversion.

'Tell me about their fathers.' She is shocked to be asked but decides answering may help.

'The first was when I did not know that you did not need a man in your life. The second is when I changed my mind but that didn't work out either. How about you?'

It is one thing to ask someone to bare their soul but to be asked to do likewise is thought stopping. Thoughts which are normally ignored then have to avoid a collision and come to the fore. 'I suppose I avoided your first. My William was an act of kindness.' He hears this and smiles broadly. The girl just looks at him with wide eyes.

'So you don't have a man either?' This is asked hopefully, the point of an alliance is the mutual support it gives.

'Oh, I do, he's over there.' I pointed at Tom.

'Oh,' is the downcast reply. I sit down beside her.

'What are you thinking?'

'That you are a better offer than all the men.'

'Stronger together? I suppose if none will be refused we could ask to be considered as a family.'

'And what kind of employer would want us?' She very reasonably asks.

My thoughts are flowing freely. 'We are a package for any man who can handle two women.'

'Would like to.' She corrects me. We both laugh, why have I found a best friend on our last day together? This draws the attention of her daughter who comes over. She does not look happy.

'You look happy, does that mean you have sold your soul and mine?' This was an incisive remark and my new friend really does cry this time, so I speak for her.

'You should say sorry. She tried and succeeded, in not doing what you said. She loves you more than that.'

'Then we can stay?' Is her hopeful question. She is answered by silence. She turns to march away but stumbles into Tom who has followed her over. A perception floods my thoughts.

Tom and the girl have a presence which I begin to notice on the other refugees to a lesser degree. They look like descendants of the hunters who arrived here ten thousand years ago. They feel they belong here and are loathe to leave. My ancestors arrived here only half a millennium ago. I only have one tie to this land and the knot is loosening.

I know what I have to say. I address Tom, 'we haven't discussed leaving because this is your domain. I knew I could not leave you on your own.' Tom is still holding the girl, tenderly. I look at her, 'I trained him to make love but not to love, that will be your job. You have already made a good start.' I realise it was a good decision to not call Tom 'daddy' to William, it will make tomorrow's parting easier.

I stand and beckon them all to follow me. We use a house on the peninsula which seems an oasis of calm compared to the throng in the Close. I spend my last night with Tom. I tell him that I want to take part of him with me. If it is successful then I can be a willing servant to whichever man claims me.

The others heard us and in the morning my new friend says, 'are you sure you want to go?' This is asked with a broad smile, not as a real question. My reply explains my plan.

'I don't need to pack, I have everything I need.' What bliss to have a friend who understands. Her daughter is listening and does not understand but thinks she ought to.

'You two are speaking in riddles and seem happy to do so. I've never seen you like this mum!'

She replies with her last piece of advice. 'Remember this moment, when you are ready you will understand it. I'm sure Tom will wait until then.'

There is nothing to pack since anything useful will be appropriated. The boats have arrived on the high tide and can only stay one hour. Tom and the girl have come down to the quay and are offered passage on every boat. As each boat fills it sets sail. The crowd is thinning and not every boat will be full so we have a choice, although limited.

I nudge my friend and she follows my gaze. Towards the end of line one of the owners is not advertising, making promises. He has accepted two families, they are not alliances but real mothers and fathers with six children between them. As we approach I can see the brand on his neck and know I have made the right choice.

We board his boat. 'Hey! I haven't chosen you.' He seems slightly startled.

'No!' I reply, 'we have chosen you.' He has no time to argue because the ebb-tide horn sounds and he has to make way. William has never heard an engine before. His first response is to hug me for reassurance. When the boat moves and Tom waves to us from the shore he is torn between sadness and amazement.

Until now I have been in control of my emotions with necessary activity suppressing them. Tom and the girl looked forlorn as the only ones left; William looks up at me for an explanation and all I can do is cry. My new friend holds my hand and her young daughter says to William. 'Don't worry, grown-ups do that all the time. I thought your mum was different. It's nice that she isn't.'

I smile through my tears on being told I am normal. I ask her mother, 'is there anyone left?'

'A few who are too old. Their families will have stocked them up with wood and other supplies for the winter. There are a few, like your Tom, who are staying to care for them.'

'We can't let them just fade and die, they need to have hope.' What I really meant was that I needed hope, for them. She reassured me.

'I expect they will all migrate south to Salisbury in search of company.'

Progress is slow. I begin to wonder if our boat will make it across the open sea. We turn left at the Isles of Wight where all the others go straight on for France. When I query this, I get the reply. 'They all want a good price. Since this is the last time I've decided to go somewhere special.' We are witness to the end of a civilisation. The coastal towns and cities still have some remnants of buildings clear of the water. Stronger structures may hold up their wonky neighbours. The giant cranes of Southampton are strewn as if by a child.

At Newhaven we turn inland, navigating the flooded land is safe if you have something to follow such as an old river. It is strange to look down on the town abandoned generations ago. The roofs are gone, the remaining walls seem like the skeleton of a prehistoric monster, picked clean by the fish we can see. Further inland we turn to follow an old railway line. The water is shallower and not open to the sea. When the captain cuts the engine the tranquillity is complete.

'I suppose you are all wondering why we are here. This is my ancestral home. My grandmother told me about it but only stories from her grandmother. It is her grandmother who is buried in the churchyard down there. So in only a handful of generations we have destroyed the world.' He restarts the engine and we continue in the same direction, here you can almost touch the submerged houses. A church tower is home to some seabirds which regard us as trespassers.

The land falls away and we are in the open sea again. I go to talk to this man who has my future in his hands, which are now lightly controlling the wheel. He has shown his humanity and so it makes sense to connect. 'I was born in Salisbury. I grew up with tales before the floods. Do you think the snow will melt next year?' Our parents used to talk about the weather and old habits die hard, but this was a serious question.

'It was all foretold, but not the rate of change. We needed

a thousand years to adjust. Do you remember the darkness?'

'I was only a child, like my son William.'

'Iceland was erupting. I knew it was time to leave. I got my brand and found myself coming back year after year; delivering food in return for whatever could be pillaged from these islands. My owner moved south eventually and left me the boat.'

'If you came so often why did you never say hello?' I ask to lighten the mood. He raises an eyebrow.

'How have you survived these last years, your boy looks healthy enough. Life is almost as hard where we are going.'

'When the land is empty there is plenty to forage and my man is a good hunter.'

'So where is he now?'

Night has fallen and I imagine him lighting a fire. Maybe his new princess has caught a duck, she has the stealth for that. He will be falling in love. I turn this fancy into words. 'He will be feasting as befits the King of Salisbury.' This draws no comment as we turn towards a light on the horizon.

I calculate that he must have been awake long enough to want to sleep. 'I will wake you when the light is nearer.' I offer.

'Do you know what to do?'

'No, but I'll keep the light in front of us and wake you when it gets somewhere meaningful.'

He stood me in front of the wheel and stooped to my height. 'When it is above the window, thank you.' With that he settles on a couch and is asleep. I look around and realise I am the only one awake. For three hours I am in a different world; in control of my own destiny; guiding us towards a point of light. When I wake him he is momentarily in another place and then reality returns and we resume our roles.

He guides the boat to the left of the light and the boat slows down. He explains, 'we have to wait for daylight to navigate around sunken structures.' It is a nice feeling to be considered worthy of an explanation.

'What will happen when we get to Paris?' I ask without

thinking but add quickly, 'where are we going?'

'Mons. You have to decide what you want. I was traded. I am not a trader. I catch enough fish to survive and exchange. You will have to fend for yourself. I expect you will all go south and then your problems will start.'

'You mean we will be free?'

'There is no such thing. Everything is owned by someone, even the wind.'

I will understand that sentence later. 'Why did you come for us?'

'There is a need for two families. If we don't replace those who leave then our settlement will die. So I came for them, not you.' He gestures at the other passengers. It is my turn to sleep. I am woken by an excited William.

'Mum, we're nearly there.' For the last few minutes we glide past a desolate scene. Artificial islands with pyramids on each. Made of stone they would have been one of the wonders of the world; but they are an agglomeration of the things no-one wanted. As a girl I had watched all manner of things being loaded on to barges for use elsewhere. This was obviously a place where they had been processed before moving south.

I wish I had William's eyes, he actually regards them as wonders but I am wondering how desolate life may be here. There is a small crowd to greet us. The families are dazed by their welcome. Houses are ready to accommodate them but the magic is hot showers. I can see some turbines turning on the hillside. 'Who owns the wind?' I ask.

'Here he comes now.' Careless of pedestrians an electric car approaches. I have guessed that the captain is about fifty. The driver of the car is not much older but twice the size. Owning the wind obviously entitles you to the lion's share. He comes straight to the point and all those nearby will hear.

'Did you find me a woman?'

'No.' This was said firmly as if he would never do such a thing.

'Then who are these two for?'

This was a more difficult question to answer. 'They are stowaways,' is the non-committal answer.

He approaches my friend, she is terrified. He is a head taller than any of us but it is his appraising look which is the most menacing. William is the only one willing to do anything. It would have been brave if he had been aware of fear. He runs at the man and yells, 'you keep away, you monster.' I suppose William has only ever seen lean, hungry men. It has no physical effect on the man but he turns to me.

'I don't want a woman with children, especially one like that. You're my second choice but you'll do.' I hesitate, looking at the faces in the crowd. He calls over his shoulder as he ambles back to the car. 'Don't keep me waiting!'

I give William my best 'hide and seek shush' and follow. In the quiet of the car I can hear his laboured breathing. What will everyone think of me, I can see comments being made as we drive away. I feel sure William will be safe until I know my situation. We arrive at a house which is far bigger than necessary and feels unloved.

I begin to think he feels unsafe showing any consideration. 'My last woman left in the Spring. Your room and clothes are upstairs on the left. Make yourself at home, have a bath.' His delivery is functional. I do as I am told. Does anyone else in the town have this luxury, I wonder. The bath is long, it could have been designed for the man but it is old with worn enamel. Was everyone taller in the past. I wiggle my toes which makes gentle waves over my weightless body. It gives me time to think. None of the clothes are suitable to be worn outside but there are some very nice cloaks for that. Obviously when I arrive in the town dressed this way I will become separate, unlikely to befriend.

I choose to be provocative and cover up with a coat which caresses the bare areas of my body. I make my way downstairs and present my new self. 'You can't be cold, surely,' is his opener.

'Obviously not, I have this lovely coat on.' The house is exceptionally warm, a perk of owning the wind. I removed the coat and was pleased to see he was surprised. 'Good, nice to know I'm your first choice now. If I'm going to be your housekeeper I will need something more practical than this to wear.'

'Electricity is necessary for survival here. I can have whatever I like from the town, they are in my debt. That is usually the food you will get for us. Just let them know what you need.'

'I'm glad you said "us". I'm going to need a couple of weeks to fill out and do these clothes justice. In the meantime I'll tidy this place up. I will invite my friend with the unruly children to help, as long as you promise not to change your choice when you see her after a bath. Children can be taught to behave and you need an heir for all of this. In fact a house this size needs two women to look after it.' He did not argue with me. He was looking at me the same way he had surveyed my friend earlier.

I wrap the coat around me again, maybe I do not have a soul to sell. I make sure he sees my expression so that he thinks he owns me. In three weeks, if I am carrying Tom's child, I can safely assume the role I am currently pretending. Safe in the sense that I will feel in control; if not will I have the will to run away?

I begin to wonder how I will be regarded. It is a long time since I have been part of a society. I want to be more than just the concubine of a despot. How would that affect William. I take a risk and ask. 'How do you come by this way of life?' He sees through my question.

'You mean, how do I get away with it?' I nod. 'I saw the look on your friends face. At least that boy was honest in his reaction. I haven't always been a monster. I control the electricity; it used to be automatic; I was a hero to keep it going when no-one else knew how to. I keep choosing the wrong women, maybe they choose me.'

'You're safe now because you chose me.' I need to keep reminding him of that. I may have is eyes but I need to know more, the better to navigate my future. 'Why did your last woman leave?' My choice of words shows I know my place.

He continues his thinking. 'They take what is on offer and always leave for something better. The clothes you found upstairs tell the story. I did not choose them. Every woman thinks they have to seduce me to maintain their position.'

I break in. 'That is obvious by the way you looked at my friend and then me.'

'Would you have followed otherwise? I don't think so. I would have been your last resort.' Self-deprecation becomes him. Thoughts are forming somewhere in my head but they are suppressed by the question; why did I follow him? I have not broken his train of thought, he wants to show me the world from his point of view. He wants me to understand how he came to this.

'When I was young I could have any woman, I did not have to try. Imagine when I was your age, every boat would have someone willing to replace you. I don't seem to be able to offer a child. As you observed I need an heir but you as my woman need one for security. Your predecessor put up with me for over ten years. I told her I would accept any child she produced. She tried but then preferred the child's father. You can only love so many times before you cease to believe. I never branded any of them.'

This troubles me for obvious reasons but also - have I ever loved? I was willing to leave Tom. Does it mean I loved him differently to how women and men are supposed to love. Should I continue to judge this man whom I do not really know. I continue with my line of questioning which springs from my original dislike of him. 'That describes you but why do people let you be so horrible?'

'I am the apex of a pyramid, it gives those below license to be the same to the refugees.'

'But that is crumbling, there are no more to come. I am the last.'

'Don't you think I know that. For the last six months I have been imposing on others for the basics. It's my fault that two families left.'

I make my final pitch. 'If I tell people that I think you are a nice man, you will have to be.' He eases himself upright to wrap his arms around 'us'; I feel the coat has a personality of its own. If he had suffered the same privations as everyone else; eating to stay warm rather than to excess; he would be handsome. I can hear his breathing again and it is not excitement.

I start to think, what if he has a heart attack. He takes my look of concern as a sign that I may not detest him like all the others. The suppressed thought surfaces; I am not a beauty but he is not a beast. He begins to smile, deeply. His arms are comforting not searching. His paunch seems to mould itself to me. 'What are you thinking?' I ask.

He replies, possibly clairvoyantly, 'with you, I can die happy.'

## Mission Paradoxical

'Is it true that you are his grandson?' She asked, slightly awestruck.

'More than three questions proves you are not ready for the mission, but I won't count that one. To answer: yes! His fame, as the man who developed time-travel, meant I had no choice but to do this job. Now here are your instructions,' he said, getting down to business.

'We are sending you back over one hundred years towards the end of the second world war.' He gives her a picture. 'Memorise his face, you cannot take this picture with you. He is six feet tall; a hint of ginger, otherwise blond; probably the most handsome man in any group.'
'You will arrive at your location at night. We have found an empty house nearby.'
'Stay in all day and leave at sunset.'
'Your contact will be in the pub on the corner. If anyone is surprised to see you emerge from the empty house, just say "bloody doodlebugs."'
'Use your London accent.'
'You will attract attention when you enter the bar; go straight to get a drink.'
'The landlady will be appraising you, so you must say, "I'm not what you think, just wondering where the life is round here. I got bombed where I was".'
'Put these clothes on, let's see if you look the part.'

She welcomed this break and went to change. On return she displayed how she had used one of the items. 'I wasn't sure what to do with these.' This allowed her to check without actually asking a question.

'You got it right, but don't do that in public!'

'Here is your bag: ration card; identity card; money. Remember you were bombed out, so are lucky you always carry them.'
'Put on the headscarf and tuck your hair in.'
'When you have made eye contact with your target, take it off and shake your hair free.'
'Don't lose eye contact!'
'When he comes over to you, loosen your coat.'

'How do you know he will come over?' To her this was an obvious thing to ask.

'Every man will want to, but he will be the most confident. He is American.'
'Use you New England accent.'

'Why?'

'Second question: the answer is he will be disarmed.'

'Are these men so predictable?'

'I hope so! That is your last question.'
'At some point you can mimic his Texan drawl. Your mission is to keep him entertained until eight-thirty. You have a story we have created for you, but we think that if you keep asking about him, he will be happy to oblige.' Obviously she wanted to know, 'why eight-thirty?' But wanted to go on the mission far more so remained silent.

'No more questions? Good, then you're ready to go.'

They went to the delivery room and a technician was ready. She climbed into the antique wardrobe and with the click of a mouse she and it were gone. The technician said, 'I haven't been given return coordinates.'

'There are none; I am still here, so the mission was successful; that was my great-grandmother.'

# Paradox Lost

It is the smallest things which change your life. We were at a wedding, family feel free to say what otherwise would be taboo. It was yet another gender fluid union. Although the groom was a man and his bride was a woman you would not have known which was which if they had not been dressed traditionally. I was the sole youngster on my table. The discussion centred on when marriages started to be like this one.

It was the next youngest person, my aunt, who declared that I, Phoebe, was the problem. 'It started seventeen years ago when Phoebe was born.' It was true but that would be correlation not causation. My mother was supposed to take the bait of this outrageous statement. They were close sisters and could normally be relied upon to entertain with their banter.

'You know very well that artificial wombs were licensed the day she was born. Nine months too late as far as I'm concerned.' This was met with knowing laughter which obviously passed me by. The reception was informal, a sumptuous buffet but no seating arrangements. It seemed to fit the setting which was old by Californian standards. We were outdoors in a Spanish style hacienda with fine views and Art Deco touches; yes, it was well over one hundred years old.

We had a gate-crasher on our table. She was middle-aged and claimed to be related; she knew all of us and so no-one had the courage to ask what relation she was, or even her name. She was strange and was taking full advantage of the buffet. Her age was indeterminate because she had an hysterical wig on. I love my hair. I pamper it and love the feeling as it ripples when I move. So far no-one has noticed, most of the boys I know seem interested in other things. I hope that when I am old I do not feel the need to use such a bright red wig to regain my youth.

It is this woman who says the words which change the course of my life. 'What you really mean, Lucy, is that Phoebe is the last real woman. Just look at her.' All eyes are on me. 'She has the look of a film star from the last century.' There is general agreement that I would have been the one declining advances from all men. Then she looks directly at me and adds, 'you were born one hundred years too late.'

Until then History had been a dull subject but I decided to find out about an age which would have suited me. Just three years later and one hundred and thirty-one years earlier I step out of a wardrobe into a musty smelling bedroom. Time-travel has been possible for many years but not many get the chance to meet their ancestors. There is a very good reason why you should not tamper with the past.

The ability to go back became public a few decades ago. It killed any form of gambling which relied on predicting events. The experiments to go back to observe important historical moments need legions of historians to analyse all manner of things to confirm it will be safe; not cause perturbations. There is a shortage of historians.

Enrolling for History at university only needs a minimum of qualifications. You only really have to show you are interested. I chose the course which had secondment to the Time Bureau because they paid well. Their source of finance was never discussed, the rumours were that they benefited from compound interest.

Induction was rather strange. There were dozens of us second year students; nearly all women. We had a whole week of lectures on the inventor of the mechanism which made it all possible. Details of his family; father, mother and five sisters. When one woman asked why we needed to know such detail the answer showed that the question had been expected.

'One mistake will change the future, our present. This is the level of detail needed to avoid such things. We concentrate on this as an example because – if this timeline is changed the traveller will be marooned.' As an afterthought he added, 'and all of you would be doing something far less interesting.'

Following my instructions I wait until dusk and leave for

the short walk to the pub in the dim light. It is strange how the alien surroundings help me settle into my role. The skirt restricts my movement so I cannot stride. The shoes elevate me and I feel empowered but slightly precarious. Everything happens as predicted. What I did not expect is how much I am enjoying it; maybe I was born in the wrong century.

My target does indeed come over to talk. 'You must be a long way from home.'

'Why do you say that?' He is surprised by my local accent.

'You don't look British.'

'Does this fit your expectation?' I reply with a New York accent.

'Almost, but you're too well tanned to come from there.'

With my best Texan drawl I say, 'you hope I'm from your home town then.' His friends call over to tell him to share me around. All is going well; time is ticking by; I feel desired. There are five of them, all pilots. I entertain them as each one's home town girl by mimicking their accents. They start to talk of leaving and walking to the nearest cinema. They suggest I tag along. I need to keep them for five minutes more.

'I'd love to but then which one of you will make an honest woman of me when the war is over. It only has three months left.' That is a bit of a faux pas, but it is generally expected. The silence is broken by the Texan.

'That may be so, but it would still be foolish to promise anything.'

Another one says, 'you're probably right, but when this is over we'll be off to Japan so none of us can think of the future.'

I need to retrieve the situation. 'Honesty is over-rated. Tonight we forget the real world and I make a promise. I will be here each New Year's Eve until one of you comes for me.' I put my hand on the table and one by one they cover it. Two minutes to go. 'You all make me feel special but I need to spend a penny. Don't go without me.' I go to the Ladies toilet and wait. My mission is accomplished as an almighty explosion shakes the building.

The bar is emptying as I return to it. The natural response at this time is to run towards the mayhem, to help. Down the street a house has been annihilated by a rocket. The Texan takes me aside. 'Stay here no-one can have survived. You saved our lives.' He interprets my shock as anyone would when I say.

'That is where I have just moved to. Now I'll never get home.' He pulls me close and I hear the landlady say.

'Got what you wanted then!' I feel angered by her tone. I feel elated that I have saved one of these men for something important in the future. I feel at ease in my persona. I feel empowered by my knowledge of this time. I feel there will be a rescue attempt and so I need to stay in the vicinity. I face her down.

'If I was behind your bar you would have a lot more customers. Are you brave enough to give me a room. I've been bombed twice maybe you'll be my third time lucky.' She has no choice; you cannot refuse someone whose home is now a crater; especially in front of everyone you know.

So here I am on New Year's Eve; with very few possessions; donated clothes and a silver ball retrieved from a garden soon after the explosion. Obviously I am not going to be rescued, even if the organisation took a year they would have arrived months ago when time is not the barrier. As a special treat for the customers I am wearing the outfit I arrived in. I kept my promise, I have made the pub popular just with my presence. The landlady is now a friend.

'You're not going to find a husband here. You deserve better than my clientele.' Or variations on the same theme has been a common conversation recently. I will have to leave soon, being a woman of mystery with a past that I cannot talk about is getting more difficult to maintain. Wartime disruption has helped, everyone has things they would like to forget.

You can tell when a newly demobbed soldier comes in. I am therapy. They talk to me and realise that they can enjoy life again. The older married men are first back into civilian life. The landlady says that I am responsible for the baby boom. 'You may be out of their league, but it reminds them they should still be in the game.'

I do not recognise him until he says. 'You kept your promise.' He waits, hopefully, and I do not disappoint.

'California! Where are the others?'

'Aren't I enough? It's just plain greedy to want five handsome men.'

'Are they OK?' I ask this in a worried way.

'You remember how we were all silent when you made your request. We talked about you later; they all had girls at home and you made them homesick; you also made them realise how powerless they were to affect the future. You reminded them of what it could be like if they only just got there. And they have! They wasted no time getting married, picking up where they left off.'

Talking of the future made me wonder what would happen to my timeline. Someone must have decided that I am of no consequence historically. That makes me free to choose my own destiny. The chaos of war is the perfect time for people to materialise from nowhere. This man has come back, presumably for me. I make my pitch. 'So what are your plans?'

'I'm the only one left flying. I've lined up a job as a commercial pilot. My country is big, it's the obvious way to get around.' It is now or never so I say.

'It's time for New Year Resolutions. I'm going to become an honest woman and all your friends will be jealous.' I suppose my proposal is lost in translation. The landlady comes to my rescue.

'I'll make you a stunning cardboard wedding cake.' He still did not understand. 'The night of the bomb she looked like a film star; nine months here hasn't taken it all away. She needs to go with you to California to regain it all. It's your destiny, she saved your life so you can save hers.'

He makes me real. I begin to forget my origins. Our second daughter is born during the Berlin Airlift. When he returns I can see how alive he is. His company is keen for him to return to work but I can tell he is not excited by the prospect. I find him the job that thrills him and I create my own. Having a daughter every two years is a full time occupation.

It is our tenth wedding anniversary and we have a conversation which makes me realise who I am. He makes a gentle accusation. 'You've hidden the rubbers again.'

'I'm determined to give you a son.'

He caresses my belly. 'Maybe girls are easier to make; perhaps we should give it time to recover.' In those words I hear an echo from the induction lectures. My son when he is born will develop time travel and I know his date of birth. When I wake in the morning I just say, 'maybe you're right. I hid them in the usual place. We'll give me a rest until the end of the decade.' When he has gone to work I start to cry. I had found him the job which will kill him and he will never see his son.

Actions which had seemed so easy yesterday are scrutinised by the second hand sweeping up time; when the clock strikes it is judgment; have I performed correctly in the last hour. I had not paid enough attention to the theory. I was happy to pretend I was living in the near past. Soaking in the atmosphere of films, books and occasionally clothes. Now I am immersed. Will awareness of my destiny change it, make it less enjoyable.

Strangely I think I am myself; I belong here; so far I have done everything correctly according to History. I realise that being my natural self in my appointed role is sufficient. The watcher in my head hits snooze on its alarm. The decade ends and New Year is a time for reflection. What will my eldest daughter think when I announce my pregnancy?

The watcher is awake. Just to be sure I arrange for the children to be looked after by his parents and book a week away; it is after all our anniversary. He tells me that he does not need a son he is happy to have daughters as beautiful as their mother. 'But who am I to refuse if you insist?' He says every day of the vacation. Having a destiny is quite satisfying.

On our return he announces that the vacation was

allowed because he now has to go away for a couple of weeks to test something secret. I never see him again. The funeral is on the day he would have returned and the coffin is empty except for a few mementos. It is a big affair; he was well-regarded and my grief strikes the perfect tone. They think my acceptance of the inevitability of his death is pride in what he did. I look like I have lost something special – and I have – my period started on time this month.

He was a hero and his superiors are in attendance. I make a request. 'I know everything is secret. Could you send someone round who understands what went wrong to set my mind at rest. I need to know he did not die in vain.'

The children are away at their grandparents when a young engineer calls. I think he was chosen because we do not know each other. I may have met the others socially and that would have created its own difficulties. At first he is awkward but when he gets into his specialist subject he forgets the formalities of grief. He answers my questions; they know what went wrong; he was describing events perfectly until he ceased to exist.

'But why do I still exist?' I ask the watcher in my head. Every morning when I wake up I ask and there is no answer. This time he says, 'open your eyes.' He is male today and takes the form of the man who sent me on my mission. The young man is saying.

'Is there anything else I can do to ease the ache of your grief?'

'Yes.' I reply. 'Make love to me so that I know that I am still alive.' I am actually thinking, 'so that I can stay alive.' I wonder if I am irresistible because he makes no objections. My husband was a test pilot who had a feeling for how machines worked. This man is an engineer who knows how they work; a rare breed. As I descend into reality I only have one thought; so that's how you make a son.

He points at the silver sphere. 'That's an interesting ornament.'

'It's a time travel field generator. It brought me here for this moment.'

He replies in kind. 'That is a beautiful thing to say. Just once is more than enough for one lifetime.'

'It doesn't work now. It survived a V2 rocket so I guess it is indestructible. You can take it maybe it is your destiny to unravel its mystery.' As he leaves I am sure our paths will cross again. My life is about to become complicated. Six weeks later I am definitely pregnant but the due date is four weeks too late. It will be impossible to maintain the lie that conception happened on our anniversary vacation.

I am woken by a gentle 'pop' sound. I am not of a nervous disposition and so at first I think I am dreaming when a middle aged man appears at the foot of my bed. 'I've arrived as you suggested,' he says. I close my eyes and prepare to continue dreaming. 'I'll come back earlier when you are more awake,' he says, emphasising the 'earlier'.

I open my eyes trying to make sense of things and ask. 'Are you a juggler? If so you should have three balls.'

'You haven't aged at all, Phoebe.' Then I understand. 'I'll be gone in ten seconds, use this to lengthen your days so our son is born on the right date.' He throws one of the balls to me and disappears; there is a gentle 'phut' as the air rushes to fill the place where he stood. There are also some instructions on the floor where he had been stood and an old financial newspaper.

*You told me not to tell you everything. You wanted free will to do what you cannot avoid. You enjoyed three extra hours sleep every night although you often watched yourself sleeping. Your grasp of the theory is beyond mine.*

The controls are quite simple and the following night at three in the morning I climb into my wardrobe. The sphere is set for minus three hours; I activate it and leave the wardrobe to lie down beside myself. Three hours later we both wake and I watch myself climb into the wardrobe. My unborn child knows nothing of this but grows in each of our bodies.

When my son is born at the correct time I am genuinely

happy which infects those around me so that they are happy for me. I start to regularly read the financial news and invest my insurance payout wisely. Theory says that you cannot go forward in time but I am already in the past so I am allowed to catch up.

Initially I go forward to read which shares to invest in. I realise that I am ageing slightly faster because I return to the time I left from; I've let it be known that I need more sleep than most people. Most nights between two and three in the morning I skip forwards. It took two years just to catch up with shortening my pregnancy. I keep a tally so that my chronological age is close to my biological one; I should have paid more attention in theory classes.

You may wonder why I use the wardrobe? Initially it was to mask the sounds of travel. They are not loud, air is quite amenable to being shoved around. It just seemed wise; later I did remember the history classes. When I was sent back I travelled in time and space but the earliest versions could only travel in time. It means you have to find a safe space to be successful; somewhere enclosed to create a frame of reference.

I place one bet. Five dollars at ten thousand to one - that a man will walk on the moon before the end of the decade. All my investments are secret, placed with multiple stockbrokers so as not to arouse suspicion. When Neil Armstrong takes his 'one small step' I am worth almost a million dollars but I live modestly; after all, six children are a full time job, but the nest is emptying.

To give you an appreciation of my secret wealth; fifty thousand dollars is about the value of my large family home. One and a half million dollars would buy an actual ton of gold. It was at this point that I started to walk into pawn shops and offer to buy their entire stock of plain gold rings. They thought that a fifty percent premium over the scrap value was a good price. I liquidated my stocks and spent the fifty thousand dollars I was known for many times.

I am a minor local celebrity. The happy smiling face of a

lucky lady is on the front page of the town journal. I am quoted. 'My husband was a test pilot who died almost ten years ago. He was doing something secret and special. I suppose I placed the bet as a memorial.' This press coverage triggered a conjunction of profound events. Henry decided to look me up.

'I saw your picture and felt guilty for a number of reasons.' No 'hi' or 'how are you'; straight in as if ten years had hardly passed.

'Come in and tell me all about it, it doesn't seem to weigh heavily on you.' He sits on the edge of the sofa looking pensive, just as he had back then.

'I'm married now.' This is a strange thing to say as I am looking my least seductive.

'To a very lucky woman is all I will say in that matter. You are absolved of guilt for what happened. I feel no guilt for using you and if my picture makes you wonder what might have been - I'll take the compliment.'

'There is also this.' He produces the silver orb, 'I could find no way into it and then forgot about it until your amazing win. I fancied that maybe you were a time traveller and those lovely words you said to me were true.'

On the table is the ancient paper he had left for me. I had got it out because it was today's; I wondered what would happen when it was delivered today. In the next two minutes actually! I gesture to it. 'Are you interested in the stock market? Travelling in time has made me very wealthy. That paper is twenty five years old but very up to date.'

He picks it up and remarks. 'This is today's news. How?' To his astonishment it disappears just as there is a thud in the porch. I feel like a magician. I retrieve the same paper, newly delivered, and present it to him.

'You will return this to me in fifteen years with a different silver orb.' Just then my son, George, comes in. They are obviously father and son; when will they realise; will they need to?

George admonishes me, 'I've fixed the Hoover, you really

shouldn't pull it by the cord. Why do they design things so they are difficult to take apart?'

I look at Henry. 'Do you tell your wife off like that? Or is she more sensible than me? I think he needs a father figure so he can be more like a child.' George has heard this before, mainly from people who should keep their opinions to themselves. This is the first time I have said it and he sees me looking at Henry.

George asks directly, 'she's chosen you. Do you want the job?'

Henry asks uncertainly, 'what will I have to do?'

'Give me interesting things to do, I'm better at taking things apart than putting them together. Though I have now mastered the Hoover.'

Henry hands the orb to George. 'Can you open this?' George walks into the kitchen looking intently at the object in his hands.

'What do you think? Can you save him from me and his sisters? We've been calling him "the man of the house" for a long time and it isn't fair to burden him; even in jest.'

Henry starts to say no. There are probably many reasons but the first is very personal. 'We have been trying to start a family for a long time now. It would feel like defeat to borrow someone else's.' I want to shout - but he is your family; of course that must have happened later.

Just then George returns. 'I wonder what it does. There is some kind of crystal suspended in a spider's web. Whenever I move it resonates with the other structure.' Henry is startled but I am just glad the stars have aligned. I have achieved what was ordained just by being myself. How special am I?

Henry's wife, Jane, becomes a friend, in fact my only friend. It is only when my youngest daughter leaves for college that I realise all the others are merely acquaintances associated with the children. George often goes on interesting excursions with Henry. He is old enough to call on them himself but today I need to talk to unburden myself of some bad news. I can see that Jane is in a similar situation.

When we are alone I come straight to the point. 'I hope your news is not as bad as mine.'

'We got confirmation,' she sighs, 'we'll never have a family. It takes away the lustre of trying.'

'But Henry is so good at it.' She gives me an appraising look. 'Did I say that thought out loud?' I ask.

I am sure she is smiling inside. 'Yes! I knew you were connected, but how?' Now is obviously the time to tell her the circumstances. 'So Henry already has a family. I'm not really needed.' She says this with an air of despair.

I have navigated my mission here by suppressing knowledge of what is to come. It bursts through. 'You are essential – I am going to die. That is my bad news; I also got a confirmation - my lump is what I thought it was. I have at most one year of life. You and Henry will adopt George and you will be the most important woman in History.'

She is appraising me again, what did I say this time? 'That was a lovely speech but it only makes sense if you can see the future. Your moon bet shows that you may.' I take a deep breath.

'It is the past to me. I came from that future. Henry and George will make it possible but you will hold it all together.'

'And where are you in all of this?'

'I have to die, obviously.'

'I can't imagine why anyone would say that, aren't you even going to try and fight the cancer?'

Bear in mind that I have only just realised my destiny; my words are emerging from a thought process which has been fermenting in my subconscious. 'I have to die so that I can exist.'

'You clearly believe this and I know how proud you are of your hair. People will think you vain if you value your hair above your life. Follow me.' We go upstairs to their bedroom. 'I'm going to show you that losing your hair is not the end of the world. You ought at least to want to live longer.'

She explains, 'I have a large collection of wigs. I met Henry at a fancy dress party and I was wearing a ghastly wig. For years I would dress up to let him know that I wanted him, it was our little game. I haven't needed to do it since you reappeared on the scene. You obviously meant something to him, but I get the benefit.'

There is a pile of wigs in her wardrobe, a friendly sleeping monster. She retrieves something from the bottom. 'This is the very first one, kept for sentimental not aesthetic reasons. It is full enough to hide your lovely locks.' She smothers me in it and I turn to the mirror.

I think she was expecting me to at least laugh but I was wide-eyed. 'It was me! It was me!' Is all I can say.' She is still in "cheer ourselves up" mode.

'Of course it is you. You don't become me by putting my wig on. Come to think, I'm glad Henry isn't here.'

I recover myself enough to say, 'it will be me who says the words which direct my life.'

'Stop and explain,' she almost commands. I try to and she asks questions of each statement. At the end she summarises. 'So you need to travel a hundred years into the future to perform an action from your past. You won't be here now unless you do.'

'You can see I will have to do it. All these years my only free will has been not knowing exactly how things will happen. Like today.' Then she says something which makes me wonder if she has a larger part in the development of time travel. 'You are here now so you must have done it. Can they cure your cancer in your time.' She throws me a lifeline. 'You don't need to die, we only have to think you have. If you choose to act in the spirit of destiny only, then only I will know. Just leave me a clue as to where you are.' That was the end of any deep conversations. The rest of the day was one of the happiest I can remember. I was going to avoid my destiny and still fulfil it. Somehow!

Phrases you may expect to be able to use without ambiguity become unusable. I start to define time relative to myself. In my youth verification is usually via DNA profiling. This is deemed more reliable than anything else. I perform my cameo appearance at the wedding and then go to get my cure. I have money because I have some good condition antiques which

I brought with me; I am not a registered time-traveller so they must be genuinely old.

There is no handbook for time-travellers. There has to be some frame of reference between your start and end point. Toilets are one of time's constants. Many buildings change over the course of their lives but moving the smelly plumbing is low on the list. Always travel to the early morning is another good piece of advice. That was when I travelled to that wedding in my long ago. I remember that my younger self had looked disapprovingly at the heap of food I had selected. I now know what the most important advice in the non-existent handbook would be – always take some food.

Rather pleasingly my biological (DNA derived) age is five years less than actual, forty rather than forty-five. The nurse who cured me was willing to believe that it was a clerical error which had my age as seventeen, and changed the record. Now that I am back in my now I just need to appear to die. In the future I had scoured the records to find a tragic accident that I could be part of.

Here I am on flight 959; in my carry-on bag I have the uniform of an air hostess; in three minutes this aeroplane will fall from the sky. I leave my seat and shut myself in the toilet. This may have been difficult to plan but that is nothing compared with walking past these people. Some are happy; others bored; a few are musing on clouds. The calm crew are relaxing; just another day. Before I enter the toilet I look down the plane and the sight will haunt me in five minutes time.

I have set the timer for minus twelve hours and six minutes. That is when the crew had disembarked the previous day. What did they do with their last evening alive. I had not watched to see if I emerged after them because I needed some jeopardy in what I was doing, I am in the uniform when the plane lurches; there is a collective gasp and I activate the unit. I step confidently out of the toilet and survey the empty seats. I see the ghostly heads of my fellow passengers as I walk down the aisle with an ever quickening pace. What have I become? No-one should have to bear the responsibility for what I have not done.

I compose myself and walk from the plane following the crew in the distance. I now do not exist. Using my maiden name I have created an identity and bought a property in a remote part of the state. I have lived eighteen months in the last year to get to this point. I am still here so the future must be intact.

My will is simple. George gets the house with the condition that he does not sell it for twenty years and maintains it for family purposes. The actual reason is that I will need to be visited from it in a dozen or so years. There is money to be divided equally between the girls. I ask Jane to look after George and hope the contents of a blanket box in my bedroom is adequate compensation.

My new home is empty. Imagine, I can create time for any purpose but, lost in the planning, I had not confirmed delivery of the furniture I had ordered. The previous owners had left one bed and that is where I lay shivering when I was startled by a cuboid 'pop'. I recognised the wardrobe. An old woman emerged.

'"Leave me a clue." I said. Fifty years ago you had a lovely memorial service. To be honest I'd given up looking; we were clearing the house. I suppose you thought it was obvious lining all the drawers with property pages.'

'Jane!' I exclaim, 'what happened?'

'I thought you'd already know.'

'But it only happened yesterday, and I've been nowhen since then.'

'Well, I'm here because we figured out how to travel and displace. Just like when you first arrived. Your house fell into disrepair and no longer exists. It was a risky manoeuvre to get here. You didn't stay long but we don't know why.'

'Does George have a grandson?' I ask this because it is the final part of my mission.

'Why do you ask that? I want to thank you for giving me your family. I am great-grandmother to a lovely girl; just taking her first steps.'

'When have you come from?' I ask this and her answer

troubles me. 'I'm sorry I cannot offer you anything will you be coming back later?'

'Thanks but I can't stop anyway, this is a prototype.' She closes the door and with a 'phut' the wardrobe is gone.

I may be asleep but the voices in my head are real. I am on a mountain top listening to echoes. The words are from the wedding that I attended twice. 'It all started when Phoebe was born.' I wake and know that I am the problem. My perturbations in time cause the most fundamental changes. Everything appears the same but some boys are born as girls and vice versa. They grow up confined by their timeline. They have to be gender fluid because the pipework does not change.

I know now why my house fell into disrepair. Somehow I will repair the faults I have created. I decide to act so that I do not have time to think about what I am doing. I fully expect to not exist when I have completed the diversion of History.

It is only one week later that I am walking down familiar streets; past the hole where the rocket had landed the night before. When I enter the pub I know immediately that this has not happened before. The scene is familiar. I am behind the bar trying to understand the accents, the money and the banter. I approach my younger self and in an accent we both can understand I offer half a crown.

'When you have a breather, fix yourself your favourite and the same for me. Keep the change.' When I come over to me I know I will be believed when I ask myself.

'Are you the rescue party?'

'Sorry I took so long. When you get back they'll find ways to deny anything you say.'

'Was my mission so secret?'

When you are conversing with your younger self you know exactly what you would like to hear. 'Have a long think about what you would like to do and I'm sure you will achieve it.' I then showed her my silver orb.

'Aren't they illegal?'

'This is the original, from the archive.' I knew I would

have to explain this because I know that I do not know it. 'It works with a local field and cannot displace so we have a long walk. I'll stay until closing time, wear the clothes you came in.'

As we leave the pub I say, 'the landlady thinks that you're my mom, so I told her you'd come for me.'

'I expect that's why you were chosen for the job, someone who can act. By the way we know you were successful.'

'I've decided what I want.' The next two hours as we walk towards and through Central London are going to be unusual. Maintaining a conversation with my talkative younger self will be a strain. The next words confirm it. 'I'd like to be you.'

'What if you were me?'

'Well, it must be fun; going anywhen; solving problems. You must be special to be allowed such freedoms.'

'Obviously I can't tell you anything because it will be confidential, as your excursion will be. Instead tell me everything which happened.' This passes the time especially as I prompt ever deeper revelations. I am surprised that I preferred the Texan to the Californian. My sense of humour has also been dulled by the years so that I find myself more entertaining than I remember.

We finally arrive at the Public Conveniences in Hyde Park. 'What do you think? I visit these places a lot. Now, you were out of sight for three weeks whilst you were being prepared. The best I can do is New Year's Eve. That's a week before you left. I'm sure you'll think of an explanation. Think of it as a week to be whoever you want to be. You look like you're ready for a fancy dress party, I think you'll blend in. I'll come with you and then travel on.'

What follows is unexpected. I do not know what should happen but we can't both exist. Since I have diverted my timeline I expect to cease. The 'pop' of our arrival echoes from the tiled walls. My younger self is keen for more adventures. 'Well thank you for saving me. Will I ever see you again?'

I almost say. 'When you look in the mirror.' But that would be silly and on reflection you never see yourself as others see you. I just mumble, 'unlikely, enjoy your life.' She should be entering a world which is completely different from the one she left. How would I have fared arriving dressed as a femme fatale from the previous century.

When she has gone I return to that other New Year's Eve when the Californian showed up. The landlady recognises me, after all I am dressed exactly as I was nine months ago in her eyes. Perhaps I am a good actress because I say. 'Phoebe asked me to come just in case any of the Americans showed up.'

Rather pleasingly the Californian mistakes me for my younger self. His disappointment is obvious when I turn to face him. We have the same conversation as before but he leaves for a different life. Still I exist. I need to think and sleep. I go back to the days before the rocket where I know there is an empty bed.

I have lived through a period of enormous change. When a man walked on the moon anything and everything seemed possible. When time-travel became possible the world must have stopped developing. There was an obsession with the past rather than the future. When I was a girl my great grandmother would have understood the world I lived in, the same cannot be said of my daughters.

Previously I have experimented to see how far forward the orb will let me travel. The wedding venue is where I found it was determined by my age. Very simply, every day I lived the end date moved forward a day also. I become a thief. I gradually move up to date in the changing rooms of a well-known department store. Finally in clothes which were fashionable a decade earlier I emerge one week before the end date; except it has not moved from the day I cheated death.

Fortunately there had been a fashion for hats so my features are obscured. A bus glides silently past me with my picture on it and the words. "Another mystery for Phoebe the time-travelling detective." I am a film star and on television in this country promoting the sixth of a successful series. Time travel as a reality does not exist but I am a well-known fictional traveller. In one interview I say, 'I have so many engagements before I leave next week that I wish I had a double.'

Research is difficult when you have a well-known face. My main source is a celebrity obsessed magazine. I have had a very similar parallel life. Five daughters and a son; all born naturally. This makes me unusual as most women now use the artificial womb. There are rumours that my son was the result of an affair with a film set technician. My husband is a commercial pilot who stood by me despite this.

By rescuing myself I had indeed stopped time travel becoming reality; except I have an orb which allows me to go back and forth up to the day I should have died. Obviously I must destroy the orb and one of my selves. At the appointed hour I am yet again in some toilets. This time at the airport where my other self has just boarded a flight to LA. I have the silver orb in my hands. I set it to go forwards zero seconds. I flick the switch

I am expecting our timelines to merge. I am the one who is living on borrowed time and who no longer belongs here, anywhere or when. The orb disappears. Simultaneously there is an explosion on the runway.

No-one sees me leave, they are all engrossed passing the news by word of mouth. Euphemistically the flight to LA shows as cancelled, along with every other. It seems sensible to retreat to the corner of a restaurant and linger over a coffee. A tide of people are washing up against an impenetrable wall made real by the departure boards. Time is driving them here; just as water is pulled by the moon, schedules are relentless; but time has stopped for these travellers and the human tide recedes.

Swimming against this current are those who have been affected. They are in shock. Just a few hours ago they had said their final goodbyes. It has been a long time since my future was unknown. I leave my table and walk towards that unknown.

'Mum?'

The young woman who questioned me thus, I recognised from my researches. My flicker of recognition is enough for her to pin my arms to my side. Squeezing me to check I was real. 'How? What happened?'

Will I have to deceive for the rest of my life? 'I wanted to travel incognito so I went to get changed. Someone stole my bag.' Never say more than you have to.

My daughter calls someone and starts, 'you'll never believe it...' I hope that someone will one day. She ends the call and finally breathes. 'Dad will be here soon, his flight was cancelled.' She is looking at every part of me, checking that I am not a ghost. I learn something about myself when she asks. 'You always did live in another world; how can you be so calm when you have just cheated death.'

I do not need to answer because a man is running towards me ignoring the decorum which is normally associated with his uniform. He checks I am real by picking me up and spinning me round. He must have done this before because he knows exactly where to hold me to make it exhilarating and secure. All I can say is, 'again'.

I wonder if, or how, I will tell him that I am not the woman he married. Time travel only exists in fiction. I have created a successful trilogy which starts with 'Mission Paradoxical' and ends with the demise of time travel. I never did tell my husband, he knew straightaway that somehow I was different. Circumstantial details in the films were changed. He recognised himself because some of the dialogue was personal. In particular in how he makes me feel alive.

# Decorating

We have lived here long enough to have decorated the whole house. I like decorating, peeling back the years. This house is the one to live in forever. Redecorating will be filled with memories, peeling back our years. We are down to the last room to put our mark on. We had brightened (lime green) the bland walls of one room when we moved in. How else do you say. 'This is ours now?'

*When I told my wife we were moving to a new house on the edge of town, she did not at first believe me. I had to show her the foundations and plans to convince her. We conceived our fourth child, a daughter, that evening. She was the first to toddle into the house on moving day. We were getting desperate for the space by then but it was worth the wait. My wife had chosen the ornamentations and it gave the downstairs a very grand feel. However, I had prepared a surprise for her in the master bedroom.*

You have to make sure you have everything before you start. B&Q may be open until eight, but when you are working and reading bedtime stories, that is when you start. I am beginning to regret my choices. Painted woodchip is a devil to remove. I know it can hide many sins but I already have a few hours of plaster repair to do. I am being more careful now. My wife comes in to remind me that we have a bedtime too. This is just as I complete my most successful removal. I am staring at the wall. Part of the plasterwork was a heart with 'I love you' set into it.

*As I looked at the finished version I wondered about the tradesman who executed it. Was it just a job, it certainly looks like it contain feelings.*

'I know you do.' She said as she came in. 'Sometimes it is embarrassing just how much. We'll have to cover it up.' I pointed to the hook above.

'I not only love you, I also know you. That is where we will hang the mirror.' She had put her arms around me and whispered in my ear.

'When I look in the mirror, I will see all the way through it.'
'What are you going to do. You can't cover it up again!'
'I don't want to.' I say, 'it will be our love from now, hidden, in plain sight.'
Two weeks later I am completing the decorating. As I struggle to not cover it up with new wallpaper I wonder about the person who did. The house was B&B for a while maybe that is when it was unloved. Now our discovery will be a talking point for friends and visitors. Because of the effort it took to reveal and preserve, the sentiment is mine as much as the man who commissioned it. My wife has been looking at the census and other information to find out who first lived here.

*My wife is beautiful, she looks through the mirror far too much. Luckily the house is big enough for six children.*

I suppose it is interesting to find out whose nest you have taken over but she is in a far more excited mood when she tells me. 'So you see,' she says, 'this house was made for at least three children,' as she shares her news.

## Married At First Sight

There was the usual banter in the registry office that morning.

'How many fools today?'

'Just because your marriage is a bit rocky, it doesn't mean they will all be. Still a cancellation or two will help; I bet the last ones will be delayed.'

'More time for them to get cold feet then. Especially at this time of year. Why do brides wear summer shoes for a winter wedding.'

'You're in the wrong job; more of a malevolent than a celebrant.'

'It's only gallows humour, I can put on a good face for them. In fact, this place is fantasy land and home is real. Do I really complain about my husband that much. He's not the man I married and I am a different woman, but it works.'

Lunch had to be a hurried; it had been a morning of delays. The car park resurfacing had surprised everyone, but the receptionist had good news and bad news. 'You're in luck, the next to last cancelled. Julie rang and then George confirmed it. So we should be able to finish on time today. There may be some disruption; a man in a hard hat came and said they may turn the power off briefly.'

The groom turned up very early and he looked more nervous than usual. He whispered to his best man, 'she should be here by now. It was a terrible argument and her last words were, "I may not turn up tomorrow."'

The previous wedding finished and they were ushered in. They stood there for an eternity. The corollary of 'time flies when you are enjoying yourself' was made flesh. The best man was rehearsing his commiserations; he had signed up for a stag do and remembering the ring; not for this. That kind of speech was for lost football matches not for being left at the altar.

There was the commotion of someone arriving late

and then the lights went out. The celebrant is prepared for everything and as she struck a match, 'isn't this romantic? Marriage by meagre candlelight.' The bride rushed in and took her place by the groom without a sideways glance. She put out her right hand and reassuringly found his left. He gave it a squeeze and she felt forgiven for the previous night's argument; she returned the pressure and he felt the same.

They both said 'I do' at the appropriate time and everyone signed the register. With only one candle this seemed quite mysterious as figures stepped from the darkness to perform the ritual. Each was momentarily blinded by the candle light. The final act of the ceremony is to kiss, whereupon each said simultaneously.

'Thank you shaving your beard' and, 'thank you for wearing heels.' These remarks went unprocessed because power, and therefore light, was restored.

'Who are you?' They both said. It should be noted that both stayed in an embrace. The best man and bridesmaid then took up the refrain.

'Who are they?'

The receptionist then burst into the room and froze. 'Am I too late?'

'Only if you have an objection. I did that bit ten minutes ago!'

Julie and George are still locked together, afraid of falling over. 'Hi, I'm George, George Smith.'

'I'm Julie, Julie Smith. I don't know what has happened but you're not the man I married.'

'And you're a different woman!' They looked to the celebrant for an explanation.

'Most people say that after twenty years not twenty seconds,' she looked across to the clerk. 'Have we just married Julie Smith to George Smith, witnessed by?'

'Ben' said the best man.

'Elizabeth' confirmed the bridesmaid.

The clerk concurred, 'yes, everything is in order. The ink

is dry. Congratulations.' It had been a busy day and the officials just wanted to go home. The celebrant concluded proceedings, or so she hoped.

'I don't want to rush you but there is nothing we can do about it now. You'll be able to arrange a no fault divorce fairly quickly.'

George found his voice, but only briefly, 'no fault!' He squeaked.

Julie had already decided to keep calm; it could have been worse; she could have married her fiancé. 'Come on, husband, whisk me away to paradise.'

As they left the celebrant opined, 'they'll see the funny side one day. After all, you do expect the bride and groom to look at each other in the ceremony.'

Ben, as befits a best man, had organised the evening. To please the bride, who was not there, it was frugal. 'Welcome to paradise,' he said as he led them across the road to a local hotel. He went to the reception and came back with a room key. 'I had already booked one room for Mr and Mrs Smith and they are otherwise full. We can have dinner whenever we want. I suggest we have a drink, eat and then carry on drinking. George's suitcase is already in the room. Have you got one?' This was to Julie.

Elizabeth had been pulling a small case, 'other George said you were going somewhere warm so you would need very little.' Ben was already at the bar ordering drinks.

'I didn't know what you wanted, so here is a selection. I suggest we each have two before we start to talk.' This turned out to be very good advice. George was the first to unravel the day.

'What has a beard got to do with anything?'

Julie choked on her wine so Elizabeth elaborated, 'they had an argument which started with her suggesting he trim his beard for the photographs. It then escalated.'

Julie was also thinking backwards, 'why would I be wearing heels?'

Ben explained, 'other Julie is quite short and George suggested it for the photographs. That was the blue touch paper.'

'Hmmm,' mused Julie and then she burst out laughing. 'There are no photographs! It makes us both sound very superficial.'

George laughed too, 'I think we should drink to that.' They both raised their glasses. Ben was quick on the draw with his phone and captured the happy moment. 'Just Married,' he typed as he said the words. 'Send to Julie, and if you give me his number I can also make other George feel a fool.'

Elizabeth obliged, 'and here's my number too.' This could have been spoken factually, but there was an inflection in the words which carried more meaning. Ben had shoulder length hair; unusual for a man and normally held in a rough ponytail. Today he was wearing it loose; Elizabeth's words were like a verbal hair stroke. Ben did not notice, but Julie did.

'Time to throw the bouquet!' There was a single rose table decoration, in a small vase, which she picked up and passed to Elizabeth. She was mentally stroking his hair as she pulled the flower to her nose; this may explain her next words.

'My love life has been on hold because of you. Who's idea was it? To be apart for two weeks before the wedding.'

George unexpectedly said, 'Julie.'

To which Julie replied, 'George.'

Ben was the first to understand. 'You've both been living apart, "to make tonight more special", to paraphrase other Julie.' He then continued addressing George, 'I told you she had cold feet. Last night you gave her the perfect excuse to open the floodgates of what was wrong with you.'

Julie looked interested, 'since we are married, I think I ought to know what his character flaws are. Anything useful for a divorce?'

Ben started a list. 'He is far too nice, a good cook, no obsessions and'

'and homeless.' George finished. 'I gave up a house share to move in with her, when her friend had moved out.'

Julie sighed, 'that's one thing we have in common then; except I did it to save money and experience a beard. It was exciting at first, tickling everywhere, but there was nothing else.'

Elizabeth thought she should put in a good word for her friend. 'You're quite compatible because Julie likes eating. She's one of those annoying thin people who can eat anything. The only flaw is that she can sound interested in whatever you tell her; she is a very good hairdresser.' She moved her head from side to side as she showed off Julie's creation. She locked eyes with Ben as she did this, finishing with slipping the rose slowly into it.

Ben noticed her for the first time, in the sense that he thought, 'I could hold your love life'. Her gaze had emptied his mind of anything else. The next thought was alarm, 'George won't be moving out.' Mental synthesis is a discipline which needs more study, three parallel thoughts merged and he said to Julie, 'perhaps you can style my hair when you return from honeymoon.' There was an elongating silence so he continued, 'since you are both homeless you may as well have your two weeks holiday in a cosy cottage in the Lake District. I'm sure Elizabeth can lend you some warm clothes.' He nudged her under the table.

She was going to say 'ouch', but it morphed into, 'oh, what a good idea.'

Julie looked at her friend, 'you know that's not my idea of a holiday.' She could see the pleading look on Elizabeth's face, beautifully framed by the hairstyle she had created.

Ben interceded, 'it was other Julie's idea, George was far too nice to object. Still, two weeks off grid; you will either fall in love or find ample reasons for divorce. I will liaise with Elizabeth and we'll find you somewhere to live.'

Just then George's phone rang. Embarrassingly the ring tone was the Wedding March. It was the other Julie and she was threatening to come and find them to spoil their nuptials; the happy picture had particularly incensed her. The others could only hear George's replies to what was obviously a rant, this was one advantage of having a very old phone which did not even have a loudspeaker option.

'She's not my floozy, she's my wife.'

'Two fiancées is not bigamy.'

'It was all accidental. It wouldn't have happened if you had come.'

Even without a loudspeaker the next words were audible, 'so it's my fault; I'll find you and have words.' Julie had been studying her own phone. She was having a similar but less acrimonious conversation with her George by text.

'Ask her about beards.'

'Would you have preferred me to have a beard?' There was an audible silence as this non sequitur had disrupted the flow. 'I'll take that as a yes.' George terminated the call and Julie took his phone. She sent one more short message and looked pleased with herself.

'I think I've just dodged a lot of unhappiness. His idea of somewhere warm was a spa hotel in Wales. I have to confess I am the guilty party of our break up. He suggested the separation but I nudged him towards it and I knew any criticism of his appearance would wound him.'

'So why did you turn up?' It is irrelevant who asked, because they were all thinking the same thing.

'I just want to be married, have a man of my own. I'll be able to empathise with my customers who talk a lot whilst I'm styling. There is a common theme; they list there husband's faults and there are never any virtues. When I've finished, they admire themselves and say "but he won't notice." I need to know why they seem so happy with their situation.'

'And you thought, if he turns up, he'll do.'

'I'm not that scheming, I'm just ready; but,' she paused looking at her glass for inspiration, 'if he'll do then you definitely will do.' Men are not used to be treated as commodities, but George was still disoriented from the recent events; he picked up her logic. He had been willing to marry other Julie and this one seemed far better. She was unfazed by their situation, would she be so understanding when she discovered his faults – no – inabilities? His main virtue was readily admitting when he could not do something – better to have a man handy than a handyman.

Julie was perplexed by his silence, she had, after all, just swiped right on him. 'Are you wondering if I'll do?'

'Oh no! I've decided you're good enough – better than all the rest – in fact.' Julie did not react adversely to what could have been taken as an insult. She knew he had just swept right on her. George was wondering what he could do to move things from a virtual like to a real one.

Ben exclaimed, 'she's coming here!' He had remembered sharing location with the other Julie in case something went wrong. Ben had a double guilt; he could have prevented the whole episode if he had looked whilst they were waiting and now she knew where they were because he had not switched it off.

George became decisive; he stood and picked up the room key; he took Julie's hand so that she stood; he swept her up in the classic pose. 'Time for me to carry you across the threshold, my dear.' One of her sandals fell off but retrieving it would have spoiled the dramatic effect. That was achieved by the lift which took some time to arrive. However, the lift doors, as they slid shut, seemed to acknowledge a new phase was beginning. Their lips were coming together in sync with those doors, we can only suspect that they stayed thus sealed until the doors parted on the top floor.

At the same time an angry voice called, 'where are they?' The words were punctuated by stomps, in the sense that there was one word for each footfall. She saw Ben straightaway and marched over. 'What did you do – no – what did you not do? Who's she?'

Ben had always found Julie intimidating, but this was a different level. He decided to protect Elizabeth, 'this is my girlfriend,' the implication was that she had nothing to do with it. It would have worked, except that other George arrived.

'I got your message. You must be Julie. I see you've met Elizabeth. Has she explained what happened?'

'I don't need an explanation; it's obvious; these two are in cahoots. I expect they planned the whole thing.' How can you reply to such an outlandish suggestion, denial of a conspiracy never works. Elizabeth rather liked the persona she was accused of being.

'It wasn't easy, but you were made for each other, so I hope you are pleased.'

Julie was becalmed, so much anger with no expression. She saw the lone sandal on the floor; it gave her new direction especially because Elizabeth was looking smug. 'Every plan has a flaw, Fairy Godmother, where is Cinderella,' she said as she brandished the exhibit. George's eyes fixed on it so much that his head was moving with Julie's arm waving.

He caught her wrist. 'Julie usually wears heels and towers over me, she must have been open to reconciliation. I'm amazed at how you manipulated me so I was the one not to turn up. I never really knew what she saw in me.'

Elizabeth was enjoying her role as Machiavelli. 'It was the beard, at first it was totally exciting; but then it rewilded.'

Julie was unsure of everything, she did not feel manipulated which made it all the worse. She needed some certainty and that was holding her wrist like an anchor in storm. 'I'm in favour of a rewilding,' she thought and then realised she had actually said it.

Ben addressed George, 'where were you going to stay tonight, before your amazing honeymoon?'

'Somewhere a bit more appropriate than this for a special woman.'

Elizabeth delivered the direction. 'Prove us right, enjoy tonight and see where it takes you.' George let go of Julie's wrist and they looked at each other uncertainly.

'It would be a waste,' said one.

'Nothing to lose,' replied the other.

'Leave the shoe,' added Elizabeth

Julie tossed it aside without a care and they were gone.

'You were brilliant,' Ben glowed with appreciation. He went to retrieve the shoe and returned to sit next to Elizabeth. 'Do you think we should ring with the all clear?'

'They'll return for dinner, Julie is always hungry.' They sat there absorbing each other for half an hour. Meditation without the posing. They were both imagining their life together; made obvious by their grins. They were brought back to reality when a shoe landed on Elizabeth's lap.

'I won't be needing this, but thanks for lending it.' Julie was looking very comfortable in the hotel slippers, with an air of having just got up. 'They didn't fit anyway, and now I don't have to compromise.'

Elizabeth picked it up, 'these are my favourite pair. I think I'll put them on now.'

'Allow me,' offered Ben, he knelt at her feet and stroked the sandals onto them. 'So Cinderella, you shall go to the ball.'

# Zenith

I thought I was a guest but these last few days there has been a guard on my door. The accommodation befits my status, I can ask for anything except my freedom. We arrived shortly before the first zenith; I knew they worshipped the sun, above all else, so our arrival would seem propitious to them. Our cities are only four days apart but our cultures could be four centuries.

They seem to have equality between men and women. Most obviously, some of their warriors are women but I have also seen women sculpting and doing other building work. They have slaves, it is a worry for us that one day they may covet the productivity of our lands. Perhaps they think our women are slaves because there are things they do not do. I have been wondering about the difference between 'do not' and 'cannot'; we just teach our children differently.

Bearing children is more painful than anything a warrior may have to endure. Men have to earn the right to be fathers and our women can reject men entirely. That is the reason we are here; I and twenty of my peers have come in search of wives. Our families wished us well but did not hide how foolish was our quest.

Our reception was mixed. One day away, on the edge of their land, we were surrounded by a group of their female warriors. When they discovered that our only arms were foraging knives they did not hide their mirth. 'Not even a slave woman would want one of these men' was one of the comments I heard; I also heard the word 'sacrifice' in mumbled conversations.

Fate is our guiding principle, we do not appease gods; even so when I saw the structures they had built I was at first amazed. Then I remembered the untended fields on our journey in and thought of the folly building skyward when the earth is at your feet. Everything changed at the zenith, we were scattered to live with important families and went about unhindered. All my friends have returned home with a wife from the warrior class and two servant wives, at their insistence.

The guard arrived when I suggested I should leave. It is the second zenith today, these last three months have been the best days of my life. I could lie and say it is the amazing history of this place, or the access I was allowed to marvel at their achievements. Of course, it is the mute one who fills my imagination. She slipped into my room that first night and gave me a kiss of fire. Chilli on her lips and tongue left me breathless. Every night she visited me and every morning she was gone. I am beginning to wonder if I had been enchanted because it all ceased when the guard appeared.

The door opens and the guard is kneeling with his head to the floor. The object of his supplication enters and I know my fate. I have seen her before, carved in stone. I had spent many hours admiring a sculptor at work. We have no such skill all our stories are told in carved wood; I wonder if our civilisation will be remembered as theirs will be. The artwork was of a fearsome woman with a snake coiled around her neck and hips; a jaguar head dress; a sword in one hand and a head in the other. How stone could give the impression of dripping blood made an impression on me which was probably not lost on others. I remember the artist looking away when I asked what it depicted and he mumbled, 'just a sacrifice.'

That woman stood before me now. 'You have proved your fertility and our astronomers predict that you will be a worthy sacrifice.'

'We have astronomers but they are servants not rulers. Our only belief is in the existence of fate. We accept what happens and do not waste energy on futile argument.' I think she was surprised how calm I was when I added, 'you should check, the zenith has passed in my city. Maybe my blood will be curdled, I don't expect to die today.' She turned and left so abruptly that the snake was dislodged and looked into me as she stalked away.

I watched the sun move down the wall and judged that she was away for an hour. When she returned she seemed less imperious. 'I would prefer to sacrifice them! I have a potion which will send you into a stupor; that way the blood will be pure, so they say.'

'What did they really say?'

'Fear is the real problem, no man is calm when the sword approaches.'

'I will be. I will close my eyes and think of the mute one. She would have been my queen, what will become of her and our child.' She removed her mask and shook down her hair.

'I will be the governor of your city!' The shock was on my face as my memories of her, as the mute one, faded to dust. Fate was whispering between my ears, 'maybe you will die today.' She must have decided that the least she could do was explain. There was a pause after each sentence as she decided what to say next.

'We have a few minutes before you must take this potion and I do not want you to think evil of me. I am the leader of the female warriors. You met them all when you arrived. It was they who asked me to intercede on your behalf. You would all have been sacrificed at the first zenith. They said that you looked at them differently compared to our men. It was summed up as 'you looked at them with wonder and they in turn wondered what you would be like, as lovers. If it is any consolation you are the best, you did not fear me.'

'You can stop there if you want to, those are enough words to help me accept this fate which is not mine.' I knew I did not want to hear any more because there would be no more consolation, but she continued.

'I formed a plan which the men accepted and overruled the astronomers. It has come to pass, all my women are in your city; ready to take over when I arrive. There had to be one sacrifice and you were the leader; you chose yourself. In our city if a man makes such as me with child, he is regarded suspiciously. You have achieved what no other man has, sorry. We have a potion, which the men do not know of, it stops us having children. I stopped my regularly supping.'

'Did you think that that may save me?'

'Oh no! It makes your blood more desirable to the gods. I decided that if I entered your city carrying your child, with news of your tragic accident, we could avoid bloodshed.'

'How did I die?'

'You were watching the installation of a new sculpture and it fell on you.'

'Thank you for saving me from that fate.' Her mouth opened slightly and her face froze momentarily but then she laughed. At that moment I still loved her and so I asked, 'have you ever been loved by one of your victims. You know that governors are mostly feared but queens are loved.'

Her snake was in tune with her body and it uncoiled; it was one of those which can crush you. It wrapped itself around me coming to rest when it was face to face with me. After what seemed an interminable inspection it glided over my shoulder, nuzzling my ear, and returned to its mistress. It was rippling in such a way as to make her pant, it stopped when she said, 'enough, I understand.'

She replaced her mask and became the warrior again. 'Guard! Come and sup with us, he needs a man present, for some reason.' I watched as she gave him the potion destined for me. Once he was in stupor, she undressed him and put him in the ceremonial robes destined for me. She admonished me, 'you won't always be so helpless, will you?' She then told me to dress as the guard.

I am glad that lowly guards are not allowed to watch sacrifices; women too unless they are officiating. There was blood on her feet as she approached me, she was her most imperious when she said. ' Thank you for helping, I have another job for you. I leave within the hour and you can carry my supplies.'

Mission accomplished, I came for a wife and I am leaving with one like no other.

## Sebastian

Sebastian Freeman was today Erik Withakay. His armpit length, free, black hair was the apex of a triangle which continued along his arms to either end of his electric guitar. The black effect – leather jacket, tight trousers and posable shoes was complemented by a bulbous nose – his microphone.

The market stalls were emptying of produce, huge discounts competing for the dwindling customers. When what you do has value but no price, there is a point when you must pack up and go home. Sebastian counted his givings, no notes but plenty of two tone coins. He separated the small coins, ready to shower on the homeless man round the corner. He surveyed the final offers and converted one pound into many. Two melons and two pineapples weigh much more.

As he walked up the path to their ground floor flat, his girlfriend smiled and waved and came to open the door. She had been running this afternoon and her scent was close, as was he. He was in love. He proudly placed the fruit on the table. She looked at it quizzically and then said, with hysteria slowly building. 'Well Noah! Better march those into the ark straightaway'.

She looked at his crestfallen face, so gave him the look that said he was the most important person in her life. She loved having two men in her life, gentle Sebastian and the wilder Erik.

## The Walker

It all started in Freshers' week. The third year Geography student on the Ramblers stall seemed so mature and romantic to my English Literature eyes. His description of walking the local moors made me feel like Cathy to his Heathcliff. So I signed up and turned up, on a damp October day. The minibus was left in the pub car park as we set off in search of the finest views in Yorkshire. It was actually a race - to have the longest time in the pub at the end of the walk.

The leader had to be last so no-one was lost, and I was slowest, by design. We were soon walking alone together and he gave me his hand on some of the (not very) treacherous parts. There were no views from the cloudy summit and geographical details were not the kind of small talk I had envisaged. As luck would have it, as he was helping me yet again, he slipped and twisted his ankle. A Premier League footballer would have made much more fuss. But now he needed my help and I held him very close all the way to the finish.

The whole group was merry, after the extra hour drinking. Back then I was rich, in student terms, I had a car and I could have driven him. At the Union Building I offered to help him home, a mile in the wrong direction. As we neared his flatshare his future wife came out. Suddenly, he straightened up and hobbled manfully into her arms. She gave him a nudge. 'Oh yes! Thanks Britney' as he remembered I was still there. I mumbled a goodbye. I turned and set off in the right direction.

I had actually enjoyed the walk and haven't stopped since. Especially for anyone who can't remember my name. One other change, from that day, was to roughly cut my long, sleek, blonde hair. I chose a slightly rusty red as my trademark colour and no longer get offered (or would accept) helping hands.

## The Forgotten

Grandad is old, but not today. We share a birthday sixty-five years apart. He is reliving his tenth birthday, on mine. First we went for a walk in the rain; his feet and splashes are bigger than mine. Now he is sat in the driving seat of a bus. His father had shown him how to drive it on his tenth birthday. He looks like a boy when he turns the key and the instruments light up. There are many symbols and he knows them all.

'You use your whole body,' he says as he pretends to turn the steering wheel, press the pedals and look in the mirror. He then puts air in the tyres, I am not sure the little foot pump is doing anything; the wheels are as tall as I am and look as though they could roll over anything. He feigns exhaustion.

'You can take over now. On your birthday come here and do this, just in case it is needed one day. My dad expected to drive this bus, so did I. Your mum and sister were not interested.' I am infected by his enthusiasm as he shows me how to charge the batteries; the strange clothes stored in lockers nearby and the weirdest thing of all, something which can move over the front window, forwards and backwards.

I know I am going to make a promise when he causes water to squirt on this window. Of everything we have, water is the most precious. There is a word to describe my feeling but I haven't learnt it yet; neither has anyone else because hedonism is something we cannot afford. I know that 'to waste water is a sin', but I am not religious. I still need to bargain because working the foot pump looks like a gym exercise.

'Let me drive the bus to the other wall and back and I promise I will look after it forever.' We are in a storage area, but my route is clear. I am ten years old and this is the first time I remember being trusted. Grandad is behind me but powerless if I do something wrong. The steering wheel is heavy so it would be difficult to change direction. I feel powerful, but scared, as the wall approaches at a fast walking pace. I turn to grandad and it as if I am looking in a mirror; except tears are forming on his elated face.

'Can I go backwards?'

'You have to.'

I know there is not much to returning whence I came, but I still feel skilful as I watch the mirrors to avoid mishap.

'Chloe, no-one could wish for a better grand-daughter.'

I feel I have learnt and experienced something special today. I did not think to ask why, where and what:

Why did this cavernous almost empty room exist?

Where would I drive the bus?

What event would cause its necessity?

I was a child with few contemporaries, we never questioned why we had videos of a world we never saw. Every adult knew and no-one thought about it; to do so would encourage feelings of being trapped. We were an experiment in extra-terrestrial living; sealed from the real world. It should have ended when grandad was a boy; why were we forgotten and why did we forget?

When we return grandma is preparing a birthday tea; grandad creeps up and encircles her. She looks as young as my sister when her boyfriend does the same. She sees me watching and a brief sadness crosses her face before happiness resumes. That is the first time I see that look. It can occur anytime there is happiness which I am absorbing and projecting back; a cloud fleetingly obscuring the sun.

Five years later my sister has two children and a loving husband. Mum and dad have overcome whatever separated them, but I still live with grandma and grandad. I now know what that cloud is and an eclipse is on the horizon. I decide to blow that cloud away; I start with a walk in the wind, metaphorically and physically. When I return, grandma can see I want to talk. She finds a hair brush and gently untangles what the breeze created.

'What's on your mind today?'

'I don't want you to be sad because of me.'

'I can't help it. Your future is so different to anyone else.'

'It needn't be if you tell me the secret of your happiness, how did you choose grandad?'

She has finished brushing, so goes to sit facing me, 'there was so much choice. I want to say it was love but we all want and need more.' She starts stripping away the years, I do not expect a hurried reply. Only when I put the cup of tea in front of her do the words begin to flow.

'He had no idea; the others thought they knew how to please me. I had more offers than you will have – sorry – that is what is so sad.'

'No, go on.'

'Well, it doesn't really matter which man you choose for most things in life, but grandad was a blank canvas. I could show him what made me happy and I knew he would try. Over time he became an expert and I have been happier than I could have imagined.'

'You are sad for me because I have no choice, only four boys, five if you count young Adam.'

'The sparse years were not foreseen, it's because we old folk live too long; and, your small group is an anomaly.'

'So there is more reason for your sadness?'

'They can't ask you to do it, but nearly everyone thinks it would be for the best.'

They did ask.

I convinced grandma that I was happy and, eventually, myself. I chose Adam as my life partner and we have two lovely daughters. I have four other, older, daughters; so everyone has been replaced. My altruism has rebalanced society, everyone is happy. I have a contentedness I did not expect; Adam, six girls and a job. Everyone has a job and every job is important. We grow up with this mantra, but I am the exception. With my family commitments a job was created for me; we have a library, full of paper books and I am its curator. It feels like I have been reading forever, to myself and my daughters. The books describe a world unlike our own and becoming less like it.

My job has become important. The books were selected, ten each, by the ones who started our world. They were told to select those which reflected the whole of life; so there are favourite children's stories, growing up, love and loss. I have read them all and can advise those who borrow them when their technology fails. We can no longer walk in the wind; rainy days are restricted and clouds no longer obscure the sun. Reactor number four is being decommissioned and we no longer have power for such earth-like features. Sad as I am about that: I am about to do something which is far sadder.

I have just been given two memento boxes, each the size of a pair of shoes. This is all that is left of grandma and grandad who both died recently. To me they had always seemed a single life force; so it is no surprise that they left almost together. Everything is recycled – one day we will eat food fertilised by their ashes on plates reprinted from their melted possessions. I know when I create my own memento box I may have to destroy the contents I am about to treasure.

Grandma has left a memory stick, to be viewed later, a child's bowl, which I recognise and clothing which we cannot manufacture. I wrap the silk scarf around my head and a woman I do not recognise looks back at me from the mirror. It is this woman who opens grandad's box. There is a wooden replica of the bus I have visited every year on my birthday. A short note from grandad makes me cry.

'Grandma will have saved all the important things. This bus is for the most important job that I never did. My dad expected he would do it; he will be surprised that no-one has yet. You are his replacement, literally, when he died permission was given for you to be conceived.' Underneath the bus was a laminated card – Protocol for the Termination of the Experiment. There was a paper sheet below that which must be very old because we cannot make paper.

'We all expected to be home by now. The last message from Mission Control was to stay put since there was a deadly pandemic. That was twenty years ago, but the experiment is going well so no-one mentions going home. I suppose this is home now for all the youngsters. If you read the protocol many people are involved in the decision to open the doors. I married the door-opener, the instructions are in the toy bus.'

I looked at the protocol; the circumstances can never happen. The communication equipment was dismantled for spare parts a long time ago. We do not have decision making assemblies and the knowledge that there is a door has been lost. The bus was a detailed replica, except the battery compartment was empty, which is where I found out about the door.

Everyone wants to know what is in a memento box, because you never look in it until someone dies. I kept the bus out and put my name on grandad's box. We are entertained by grandma's memory stick which we watch at mum's; she has a working screen. My children are greatly amused by their elders as youngsters. There is even a video of mum holding the toy bus, which she cannot remember. I am taken by surprise by a picture I created, which grandma thought to save. I do remember it took all day to colour the woodland scene; I used at least ten shades of green. It has been a fun evening and so it is obvious, as we get ready for bed, that Adam is worried. All jobs are important but his is more important than most.

'I won't sleep until you are asleep and you won't sleep until you have shared your burden,' is my opening line. I have my own worries that I also want to share. Eve my eldest daughter has seen my sad look; she should be thinking of boyfriends, but there are none close in age. My 'sacrifice' has just pushed the problem on by a generation. The only boys she knows live in the books she has read. His reply makes my thoughts irrelevant.

'Another reactor is behaving the same way as number four. When we slow it down it takes longer to come back up.'

'No more rainy days then!'

'No more days.'

'What!?'

'I mean, no more nights; just one long day – to have a

more constant load.'

'You just caused me to panic. It is not a nice feeling. What will it do to everyone else. Go to sleep, I will worry about it for you.' Adam is a few years younger than I; one aspect of our relationship has ossified; he always does what I tell him. How can he sleep like that when there is so much to worry about? We are taught from an early age that panic is the worst emotion and although I said I felt it, I am not sure that I did. There is a voice in the corner of my head which says, 'that is just what we need.' I obviously have no ideas but I know how much we depend on those reactors.

I fall asleep and find myself in a darkened room. I am not alone; everyone is banging on the wall; calling out. I ask everyone individually, 'help me find the door,' but they ignore me. One by one they fall silent and I am truly alone. I cannot find the door but beyond it I know there waits my ten shades of green picture.

I am shaken awake by my youngest daughter Zoe. 'Come on, mum, you're late for school.' Adam was kind enough to leave me in the land of nod.

'Is there any breakfast left?'

'None of the good stuff. There are plenty of insect flakes.' There is no privacy in our apartment. 'Will I look like you one day? Eve does already and she likes it; keeps looking in the mirror. I think she's turning into a wolf. How did you stop it?' I give her the look that says I enjoy the questions, but do not expect any answers. I step out of the bedroom into the classroom. There is no school. My girls are the only children of school age; I am their mother, teacher and friend. Eve is now my teaching assistant, she knows everything I know except for one thing.

'Today, class, we are going on a visit,' I brandish the toy bus, 'to see the real thing.' The bus is not a secret but I have never shown them. When Eve was ten years old I was carrying Zoe and the chance passed. They really enjoy the store room and the bus. I have become ten years old just like grandad. I finish the lesson by driving the bus to the far wall. Zoe had been reading lots of stories and knew what to do.

'Oh! This looks like my stop.'

'Don't you want to go backwards in the bus?' I ask.

'Don't be silly! You catch a bus to get somewhere. I'll catch the next one back.' She waves as I reverse the bus to its starting point. She seems in her own world; crouches down to study the floor; gets up and walks a few steps; retraces and goes the other way. We are all watching, thinking different things on a range from silly sister to lucky sister. I am just wishing I still had curiosity.

'There are cracks,' she pauses to see if we are listening, 'in the wall.' I hurry over, trying not to look too excited. I have moved too quickly and breathlessly ask.

'Where?' I follow her little pointing finger, as she swivels.

'Here, there and over there.' I start to look intently; Eve understands me; she was always observant but years of being the oldest, responsible for all unattributable misdemeanours, she can read minds, especially mine.

'What are you looking for mum?'

'A keypad with numbers.' After a few fruitless minutes Eve asks why? 'This must be the door.' I almost add 'obviously' but then realise I need to explain. They can all read me and obediently sit in a semi-circle, cross-legged; faces upturned. I do the same, childbirth kept me flexible.

'The real world is outside and this is the doorway to it. We should have left here when your great-grandad was a boy. Something happened outside; we stayed; we forgot. It must have been bad outside because they forgot too.'

'So you are looking for a keypad to open the door? Just like the one on our apartment.'

'I guess so, the instructions were in the toy bus that grandad left me. "Press 1,2,3,4 simultaneously to activate lubrication," is the first instruction, and then all six to open.'

Zoe stood up, 'well I'm number six, you keep telling me, so that's mine over there. You'll have to find me something to stand on.' We follow her gaze, 'BAY 6', in large letters was written on the wall. The six was in a circle. Eve went over to the number one, 'it moves,' she breathes, 'it moves,' she shouts. Without instruction my girls went to their stations and the older four press their numbers. There was a single knock on each side as something falls over.

Zoe was frantically jumping, trying to reach. 'Will you be happy if I just lift you?' She leapt into my arms. 'I expect yours is the most important one. Ready everyone? Press and hold! One, two, three, four, five, six.' Zoe gives a determined push and there is a rumble; a shaft of light; we all run to it. Would it ever stop, the vista grew and was soon bigger than our minds; beyond imagination. My childhood picture is talking and saying, 'look! I'm alive!' Sight is overwhelmed; there are ten thousand shades of green; real clouds; a watery sun creating soft shadows. When the doors stop there is silence but then gentle sounds assail us from all directions; the breeze rustles the leaves; invisible birds call. I have been holding my breath in awe of these assaults on my senses; as I breathe in there is a smell; fuller than something similar in the insect farm. I have never experienced shades of smell before and then we are touched by the chill.

'Come on, I know where there are some coats.' We go to the lockers, each size is a different colour. They are a rainbow and I am grey with a hint of colour from grandma's scarf. Every few seconds I look, nervously, to check this is not a dream. This is my destiny. Zoe is in red and as I lift the hood and tuck in her hair she solemnly asks, 'there won't be a wolf, will there?' She sees my indulgent smile and is comforted, unaware that I have no idea.

'All aboard,' I call out; a memory from a book. I have never felt like this as I start to drive the bus, properly, on a road which no longer really exists. All the trees are different; I now know the arboretum was created by the founders of the experiment. Collectively nothing is missed.

'Stop,' Eve commands, 'I think that is an apple tree.' We all get out to stare at it; Eve reaches up and plucks an apple from just above her head. She looks fit to explode as she savours the first bite. We all want the experience because it cannot be described. I am somewhere in my mind that I have never been before; I feel I can stay there forever but a scream brings me back to reality.

'Ieeee, a wolf,' I open my eyes to see Zoe quivering as an animal dances around her.

'Tess' a voice calls and it bounds away. A figure emerges from behind a bush and walks confidently towards us. We are ignored as he approaches Zoe. 'Sit!' Both she and Tess sit; he laughs; he is a boy disguised as a man. He takes Zoe's hands causing her to stand and then puts one of them on Tess. There is a background of giggles as he turns his attention to Eve. He strokes the sleeve of her coat and she does the same to him. One was made and the other grew. The experience was new for both of them. He spoke with an accent but we could understand him.

'You came out of the hill?' We all mutely nodded. 'Then, 'tis true. We will show you things and you will understand what we don't.' He took a locket from around his neck and placed it over Eve. He took her hand and simply said, 'come.' She looked to me for guidance, but only saw happiness, so she went.

'Right!' I said brightly, 'let's pick as many apples as we can.' Low hanging fruit is a reality. When there was no more we continued our excursion to the edge of the forest. Beyond, there was a large number of buildings with no visible inhabitants. More usefully there was a large circle where I could turn the bus around. The return was just as enthralling and no-one talked about Eve; it was just one morsel of strangeness in a remarkable day. As we approached home I could see the throng outside the doors. Collectively they looked dazed, slightly slow movements in random directions; bees waiting to return to the hive.

I saw Adam, my man disguised as a boy. Unlike the others he was awake to what had happened. 'I told you not to worry,' I said as I offered him an apple.

# The Away Match

It is eye-catching in its upper reaches, so, mesmerised, I turned left. Round yet another corner onto the third side, desperation was growing; to find an entrance. This was not the adventure I had been hoping for; please let it not be on the fourth side. At last I saw a door, with no handle; a woman was juggling shopping and a device; the door opened. Drawn to this portal, I, unnecessarily, held the door and followed her in.

The door closed itself and the world was suddenly smaller. The street outside was now silent and I suspected that the temperature here never changed. She sighed and glared at an empty chair. Would she have spoken had I not been there? 'He's supposed to open the door, especially when he can see someone struggling. He doesn't smoke but still has cigarette breaks.' That would be me if I worked here, I thought. I would yearn for anything to happen.

She seemed laden with nothing much but gallantly I called the lift. Her heels clicked as she walked, and I noticed she was not dressed for supermarket shopping. Her bags were all crisp card, with names emblazoned on them. They meant nothing to me but the whole effect was imperious. 'Fifty-six,' was all she said. I made her selection and then paused over the array of buttons.

'Which floor is the viewing platform?' I already sensed I was in the wrong lift, but her confirmation was belittling.

'This is the residents lift; yours is round the corner with all the paraphernalia of the tourist attraction.' Then she fixed me with a stare, which said far more than her words. 'Promise me, you will go straight back down and then out. I am supposed to call security; I will be told off and you will be treated as an intruder. It will make their day and ruin yours. They have no power really, but it is like being savaged by a fluffy…,' her words stopped as quickly as the lift.

Darkness and silence. One second seems a long time as your senses reach out. A single powerful LED glared down with all the ambiance of an interrogation room. Our conveyance was revealed as a box. The word coffin was forming in my mind but my companion was unperturbed.

'Can you tell us where we are?' This was not to me but directed above the door. I am glad my reactions are slow, because I would have made a fool of myself. Actually I still did, because I jumped when a voice replied.

'In between fifty-one and two.'

'How long are we likely to be here?'

'External power cut, so no idea.' The voice seemed inside my head.

'Ok, we'll evacuate. Cut the main power and open the doors.' She saw my open mouth get wider as the doors of the lift, and the floors above and below, did her bidding. By way of explanation she said. 'When I spend tens of millions on a place to live, I check how things work and what happens when they don't. It is my job, risk assessment.'

She took charge. 'You are the tallest,' she said, looking directly into my eyes, 'climb out and give me a hand.' It was easier than expected, the wall had embedded footholds. I had passed risk assessment, she handed me all her belongings and then herself. I was expecting her to rearrange herself but she simply removed her shoes and then her tights. I was lost for words again.

The clothes she was wearing were co-ordinated with subtle colour matches and contrasts; they seemed fitted by an unseen hand, discernible only by those initiated into the sect. It had made her invisible to my eye, but now barefoot she was beginning to exist, at least from the knees downwards.

She felt the need to explain. 'These heels are not designed for multiple flights of stairs, and these tights cost an arm and a leg.' An image floated through my mind; I started to grin. It was infectious. With the first hint that I may have misjudged her she asked.

'What is so funny? I hope it's not me!' This was asked with a smile and was not a demand.

'Sorry! I just had a vision of you struggling to put your tights on one arm and one leg.' She took a few seconds to appreciate the humour.

'For that you can have a cup of tea, and, if you lend me your sandals you can visit my viewing platform.' I carried her possessions and she ascended the stairs with a pleasing clop rather than an imperious click. I was slightly breathless from just four flights of stairs and the rest was taken away as she let me into her eyrie.

From below your eyes are drawn to that point where this building pierces the sky. If glass and steel could speak, 'I am here, and, I will slice any clouds which try to surround me.' Now here I am, looking down at those tiny people, I was one such moments ago.

I was not envious because on holiday I always look forward to viewpoints. For fully five minutes I was absorbing the view. From one iconic building to another I scanned not the horizon, because most of it was below me. The mainline station below like a child's toy. The river, hemmed in; does it struggle through this metropolis? Or, is it a sleeping snake biding its time? The recognisable buildings robbed of their mystery.

Foolishly I was giving a commentary. The woman was smiling at me 'I'm glad I invited you in, seeing my world through your eyes reminds me how lucky I am.' She had changed into normal clothes, although I suspected they were expensive, they looked worn and loved, 'and now the promised cup of tea.'

I was vaguely aware of a ritual being performed. A shelf which contained many different teas was being studied. Tentatively, one was reached for and then rejected as she looked across at me. The decisiveness of the choice and the use of a tea timer made me feel I was being judged when she handed me the mug.

'Honey, milk or nothing?' She innocently asked.

I passed the test because I sipped, before replying,

'nothing.'

She sat on a sofa, with her feet curled up. I was lost in an armchair. We both clasped our mugs because you would need telescopic arms to reach the table. She opened the conversation. 'I don't do interviews and I am not famous, so tell me, why are you here?'

'A football match, the five-thirty kick-off. So I ought to leave by four. I am not killing time, I planned this visit as part of my trip.'

She smiled at the joke she was about to make, 'you needn't have engineered a power cut just to visit me, but thank you. By the way, you will have to leave earlier since you may have a thousand steps to negotiate. That reminds me.' She reached forward to the table, like a mermaid, to swap her tea for a phone. 'Hello Emma, darling. Are you feeling very fit, your brother would like this challenge...' My eyes roamed around the room as she explained about the power cut affecting their dinner date and how she was lucky to have an intruder to entertain. She resumed her pose, 'mermaid with tea'.

'Why have you got a car bonnet on your wall?'

'Stylish, isn't it? It contains the backup power supply. Enough for a thousand cups of tea. My neighbours won't be so lucky. Risk assessment can be creative, it is not just spreadsheets and diagrams.'

'And lucrative apparently.'

'Only when you don't need the money!'

'Are you going to explain that? Or, leave me wishing I did not need money?' She was silent, pondering. 'Sorry, it's none of my business, I've never conversed with a mermaid before.' She smiled at that and looked towards her feet. 'Tell me, when you fierced me in the lift, what were you thinking?'

I think she enjoyed the reply. 'Not again! Why do I attract all the muppets?'

'You really were a different person, are they both you?'

'Emma, my daughter, is a minion in a fashion house. I am taking an interest in what she is doing. I've become a patron of those shops which don't display prices because they don't have any. If the power returns we'll meet in the restaurant this evening and I will be transformed again, by the contents of those bags you kindly carried.' That did not answer my question and I suppose I looked as if I was expecting more.

'Is your job interrogation? To be treated with respect in those shops you have to dress in a way that says you are not a time waster and equally do not want to waste time.' I think she had already told me more about herself than she wanted to, so I changed the subject, if in doubt...

'What's it like here on a low cloud day?'

'Serene.'

'And in high wind?'

'Exciting.'

'What about fog? When you are above it; it's always exciting in a cable car when you break through to the sunlit uplands.'

'They are the best days, when you wake up to sunrise over Canary Wharf and you are in a wilderness.' I got up, to better imagine it, looking eastward. I suppose it would depend on the height of the fog, delineating the members of the tall building club. The thought that the whole city could disappear except for a select few icons made me think of those jungle canopies with the occasional tall tree.

Staring into the distance was like staring through time. 'I was a minion, programming computers for fifty years; just one of the many thousands who contributed to the world we live in. None of it is magic, but most treat it that way. Your description has magic; do you think they know they are living in a wilderness, surrounded by mechanical beasts?' We were both silent for a while, and then, unbidden, she said.

'That's one of the risks of living here. I think you would be a philosopher and it wouldn't suit you.'

'What am I then?'

'Hmmm, you must already be philosophical, supporting that football team. You are an amplifier of experience. You've made me want to set my alarm for sunrise.'

'You can be an oracle with your riddles.' I turned from the view and she was thoughtfully smiling.

'You really want to hear my life story?'

'It's bound to be better than mine, maybe I will amplify it for you so that it gets better with hindsight.' She came and stood beside me.

'I was a minion too, in that office block over there.' She pointed towards the City.

'Did you ever look out of the window and dream of living in the sky.'

'You are sly, my daughter would dream that. I am back at my desk, which was not a window seat! And, accountants don't dream. My escape was a secondment. The firm was sponsoring an adventurer and I was a mole, ostensibly to help with the accounts. It was interesting; the planning; the minutiae; the risks. I was the mouse in the corner when they were discussing ropes; how many; how strong; how light. There were many competing ideas, in desperation they asked my opinion.'

'I was an accountant, trainee, so I replied, "not the cheapest and not the dearest; a bungee rope would be fun." The participants parted like the Red Sea and I was face to distant face with the leader. I think he hoped I had a reason, I had been imposed on the group and I dampened their banter by being there.'

'If the rope is for when you fall off that is what a bungee rope is designed for. Spend the money on a decent helmet with a face surround. He took my advice. After the expedition he came to thank me and offer me a job,' after a slight pause, 'over time I learnt how to see accidents before they happen.' This was not a throwaway remark, without her heels she was no longer eye level. As I turned to face her she was looking up at me, the subject of her clairvoyance.

I decided to speak, just to allow her to stop if she wanted to. 'You've preserved those memories in perfect condition, was there any dust on them?'

'No, you sent me back in time. I remembered when this building was just sky. But I haven't explained the riddle yet.'

'You don't have to.' I knew why I did not want to know, if the explanation was mundane it would spoil the moment. I was thinking, *what else does she see before it happens*, but I asked, 'what would you be doing normally?'

'I would be catching up on my online magazine subscriptions; getting ready for the evening.' My expression said, 'surely not the kind of woman who spends hours in front of the mirror.' She put me in my place, 'men are vain too, you know. I am a list person, I write them and never read them; I will jot down things to remember to say to Emma.'

'Does it work?

'Eh?'

'The act of writing as an aide memoire or is it pure WOM?' She looked at me quizzically, which was the desired response. 'You've heard of RAM and ROM, well, WOM is Write Only Memory,' I paused, 'the amount you laugh divided by the time it takes you to twig defines where you are on the nerd spectrum.'

She eventually laughed and said, 'what a wonderful concept, I've known people with an abundance of WOM.'

There were no clocks but from the position of the sun it was time for me to leave. 'Can you call down and tell them to expect me in half an hour? Tonight, if you meet your daughter, go as you are; you look far younger than when I first met you.'

'You mean I should abandon being a fashionista.'

'Yes, unless you enjoy attracting muppets.' My first impression of her had been completely wrong, I had judged her by appearance; she had judged me by actions.

I hope she enjoyed my company, her parting comment was. 'Take a break every ten floors!' Was I an accident waiting to happen? Closing the door with no handle I filed the memory to gather dust, the whole encounter had just been time in space.

Two years later I was given the answer to the riddle; towards the end of the Graham Norton Show. 'Finally we come to you Emma, wearing one of your own creations. For those of you who have been living on a different planet, Emma has turned the world of fashion on its side. Would you like to describe how it works?'

Emma stands and holds out her arms, she looks like a ship in full sail. The billowing white upper body becomes sea green at the waist and then graduates to the deepest blue at the floor. The neckline plunges below her navel with perfect symmetry, side to side and at the back as well. 'This is inspired by my brother, it shows that twosies can be high fashion.'

'Yes, the twosie! Beloved by football fans, male as well as female. What made you break with convention; to split clothes left to right rather than top to bottom.'

'It was a memorable evening, a regular dinner date with my mum. She came as herself and looked so much younger. It made me feel older, grown up.'

'Do you always talk in riddles?'

'Maybe, anyway, she had met a man in a lift, during a power cut. He had told her a joke, which she found funny and I didn't get it. She tried to explain it, but failed. In the end she said, "you're doing the right job for you, but let me negotiate the contracts when you have your killer idea."'

'Can we all hear the joke?'

'No, it's not funny.'

'So! On a memorable night, your mother tells you an instantly forgettable joke.'

'Oh! I've just got it.' Emma chuckles, 'I suppose it is funny.'

Graham waits but nothing is forthcoming. 'Private jokes do not play well on national television. Did the man in the lift have anything else to do with this "memorable" evening.'

'Oh yes, the twosie was really his idea. He had a vision when mum took her tights off.'

'In the lift?!'

'No, when they had climbed out.'

'On next week's show we will have Emma's mum in the Red Chair! Carry on Emma.' Graham tosses away his prompt card to show that he really does not know what is coming next.

'Well he imagined mum wearing tights on one arm and one leg, because she said they cost an arm and a leg.'

With a look of relief Graham interrupted, 'and the twosie was born. I've been told you created and pitched your designs for free.'

'If you believe in what you are doing you can make offers others can't refuse. Mum spends one per cent of her life in lifts so that is her favourite commission rate. Some of her contracts have been quite Faustian, for those who sign.'

'I did have one last question, which I hope it is safe to ask, how did your brother inspire your gown?'

'Oh, that's because he is a sailor – for hire.' Emma adds the last words innocently.

When the laughter has died down, Graham concludes. 'YOU are priceless, and now music. In one of Emma's creations which leaves little to the imagination is a singing sensation.'

I turned the TV off and blew the dust from my memories of that day. It felt good to think she had taken my parting advice and been herself that evening. Except who was she? I remembered a mermaid who sees accidents before they happen; what kind of Faustian pact could pay for an apartment in the sky.

## The Crossing

We should have waited, but we were desperate to get to the beach. The car in front stalled and would not start. The barriers came down around us. Women and children first is meaningless when there are no men involved. Don't panic we have at least ninety seconds. We curse the child-locked doors. Precious seconds tick by as we fiddle with seatbelts designed to save lives.

We run to safety, but where is safe? Which direction is the train coming from? Bruno barks, his eyes appealing to us through the back window. We cannot leave him. So young we have not yet trained him. We release him from the back of the car and he scampers around. We can see his harness among the buckets and spades.

Bruno sets off along the track and we give chase. What a game, he outruns us with ease. In the distance he stops, where have we gone? Don't we want to play? We can see the train bearing down on him. The horn sounds, but we cannot bear to look.

The train is trying to stop, showering us with sparks as it slides by. Standing passengers are falling over, cups of coffee too. They will be angry with us, but I'll be glad we did not die. Bruno finds us in our hiding place and we smother him with joy. One of us is later fined, but the train did stop before our car. Bruno is a hero for alerting the driver in time. We are in the doghouse.

# The Hairdresser

'I haven't seen you before, you must have had a recommendation to ask for me specifically,' was my opening line. I lifted her hair and studied the perfect folds, she really did not need my skills. I could feel my nose lengthening, I could see in the mirror that it was still normal but it seemed at least a foot long and was beginning to itch in a familiar way, I needed to know more about this woman. I have four sons and three daughters-in-law, she could be the fourth.

'My friend Jasmine told me about you, she thinks you are a witch!' I was so startled that my nose brushed her ear, and she felt it. The itch was unbearable, luckily she continued. 'Whatever you did to her hair, worked. Her boyfriend proposed.'

'Oh that! The lopsided cut which would make him see her differently. I gave her some strands to tie around his ring finger; just to give him the idea.' She looked up into the mirror straight at me and arched an eyebrow.

'You told her to tie them around when he was a asleep and say "now you are mine", sounds like a spell to me.'

'You can't make people do anything they don't want to, it's all psychology. Her boyfriend needed to be sure she would say yes.' I thought that was a plausible explanation, Jasmine is one of my loyal customers, I often help her. This woman would not let go.

'That's what I say when others at work say I have a magic touch. You'll find me at the travel agent, convincing people to choose the nicer holidays.' I could believe that, she smiled at me as she told me this. I could feel thoughts disappearing, my mind was emptying leaving me open to any suggestion. Even my nose was back to normal.

'So, have you got a man in your life who needs some encouragement? I couldn't possibly style your hair any better.'

'Eligible men don't visit travel agents, they always arrive

already spoken for. I also see faults too quickly.'

'So, you need love at first sight since love is blind.'

'You are a witch! I'm not going to forget that, I will have to stop looking at men just in case I fall for the wrong one, like Jasmine.' This unsettled me as I knew how much she liked her newly betrothed.

'You'll have to explain that.'

'She doesn't love him so he'll have to be nice to her for the rest of his life.' I could see I would have to help Jasmine in the future with a besotted spell for her husband. Knowing her, that would probably include the wedding arrangements. I had more important things to think about.

'I'm glad you only booked a consultation, because there is nothing to improve. I can take a sample for our new analysis tool.' She agreed, so I pulled hard on just one strand.

'Ow!'

'Sorry, it works best with the whole hair and you may not have agreed if you had known.' Her look said that she did not believe me but that she did not mind.

'Just don't tie it round some random man's finger.' I really could not tell if she was joking or not, but I had one in mind. My son has inherited my magic but no-one realises, they just think he is a very good plumber. He is my last hope for a granddaughter, why did I choose a man with such a strong male line; four sons and six grandsons so far.

When I got home they were both waiting for me to magic something in the kitchen, which is not my forte. I went straight to my son and pulled a hair from his head.

'Ow! What was that for?'

'Time you learnt to cook, you can start by reading the instructions on a ready meal. I have something to do.' They both looked perplexed but knew I sometimes had moments of seclusion. This spell would have been difficult for my grandmother, but she did not have superglue. It was she who had taught me the power of hair magic. At school the teachers lost interest in me when I said I wanted to be a hairdresser. One in particular was very dismissive but, years later, I still helped her get over her divorce.

The spell was quite simple, I glued the two follicles together and then wrapped her longer hair around his; with another dab of glue I joined the ends together. I reached for my compendium of fairy stories, which my boys had never been interested in, and found the perfect page. I formed a heart from my creation and closed the book tightly.

Downstairs something was cooking, 'did you let the oven warm up?' There was an elongated yesss, so he had learned something from his previous attempt. 'I need a holiday which means you have to go on one. I had a customer from the travel agents today and I'm sure she'll find you something suitable.' I used my voice which does not allow dissent but then softened and said, 'lasagne is a good choice, I'll teach you to make it one day.'

On Saturday I ambushed my son at breakfast. 'You know how you live here for free and never spend any money, today we'll go into town and you can buy a holiday.' Argument is futile with cereal in your mouth. One hour later I said a cheery 'hello' to a woman who did not recognise me, but she pointed across to another desk. Twins! My son was behind me and luckily only saw the intended target.

'Hello, after our talk I decided you were the one for my son. I mean to find him a suitable holiday, he is clueless so will need your help. Money is no object because he lives at home for free.'

I retreated to watch what would hopefully happen. I heard parts of the conversation, she started by asking.

'Where would you like to go on holiday?'

Later she said, 'there is a supplement if you go on your own.' To which he replied.

'You could come with me.'

I was being watched by the twin sister, 'you look pleased with yourself, she told me about the consultation. Would you like one of my hairs, I can read minds.'

# The Coalmine

We were sat in a bay window, catching the winter sun which glinted off the bone china cups we were sipping tea from. 'This is very genteel,' I said, using a word I had just discovered.

'That is why I called you in. You have a way with words,' she replied. She saw me eyeing the cakes, 'help yourself, they're leftovers from an earlier meeting; one of the perks of the job, I suppose.' She looked down contemplatively at the effect of that perk, 'at times like this I'm glad there are no men around to make me feel not young. My partner is still the same as when I flicked her hair; she says we meld perfectly. That is why I need you.' I must have looked puzzled and slightly alarmed. She chuckled at what I must be thinking so she clarified. 'There are no men! A long time ago most coalminers were men; we have been very lucky, in the past, enough women have chosen to do the job. I'll let Claire explain; she'll be here soon.'

I was having afternoon tea with Susannah, the National Coordinator. In this genteel way she runs the country, which largely runs itself. My mind is wandering, if she were an animal she would be a hybrid; the approachability of a pony with the speed of a racehorse and strength of a shire horse. I must stop this, I think to myself, as Claire comes in. I know she has the memory of an elephant but her thinking abilities resemble a gazelle as she moves from one thought to another.

Her first words were, 'it's worse than I thought, they are getting old together. Some should already be retired. In five years you will have shortages, and in ten a largely newly trained workforce.' I noticed the directness of 'you will need', Susannah has never been one to shirk a burden. I know these two from extended family acquaintance; in their presence I still feel like a girl.

Susannah elevated me, 'you are the only one I know who can do this and I trust your light touch. Success will mean there is no problem; no accolades; just "Angela writes such entertaining stories". No-one will know how you shape our world.' Her parting words were. 'Experience the real thing'.

I write mainly for radio but for that we need strong sound effects to create an atmosphere. That is why I am now on an empty coal train trundling through the countryside. I am soaking up the sunrise, orange rays made solid by the rising mist, if needed I will squeeze them out when I am half a mile underground.

On arrival at the colliery I wonder if my love story, set in a coalmine, was an imaginative leap too far. Anything beautiful that leapt here would be devoured, absorbed by the pervasive blackness. I am early but surprised when the dull outlook is brightened by some women, like flowers, walking in.

One petal peels away to where I am watching. 'You must be Angela. I've been told why you are here but I have no idea what you expect to find.' She leads me to the changing rooms where the team is transformed to orange flowers with yellow stamens. She hands me the same kit. They admire my dress, as I carefully hang it in the locker, much more than they admire me.

My guide hands me more clothing. 'This is my spare. The overalls chafe more than a cheese grater.' She helps me into this soft, woollen garment and then the overalls, helmet and boots. I gaze at her as she checks me over. This is the woman who keeps me warm at night. The next time the coal is glowing red I will think of her. My thoughts must be visible.

'You should leave your imagination up here, it will be a dead weight down there.' Outside a hooter commands attention. Our soprano chatter subsides and is replaced by the bass notes of our boots as we cross the yard to the lift. The scissor gates slide open and the morning shift step out dazzled by the dark colliery buildings.

We shuffle in, packed like penguins. 'Stand clear'. The gates clang shut. The descent is long and slow and our creaking box asks 'Do you really want to go?' Silent, except for the rubbing of our overalls, the intimacy of that journey melds the team. The coalface is distant. Only harmonics reach us as we sit in coal carts headed toward it. The sound swells as we near the cutting machine like music which slowly crescendos to a climax and then silence. This is an unfinished work just endless final notes, unleashed.

I am in awe of these women, their teamwork, strength and understanding. Communicating with signs my guide beckons me to follow, after a few steps the tunnel wall swallows her. There is a narrow gap to a cosy alcove, I breathe in and enter. She covers the entrance with a thick blanket and the noise speeds past unaware of our existence, we can talk.

'Lunch! I brought extra for you.' She pours some tea and bubbles into it like a child. 'Your turn'. I wonder what this superstitious ritual means. Like a magician she produces a clean white cloth and strokes my lips. The gentleness is beyond my experience. 'Put your imagination away! You don't want to eat coaldust, do you?'

She is careful not to contaminate the sandwiches which are messengers from the overworld. Silence. I feel the weight of the rock above us. Unconcerned, she says, 'they will call if I am needed. I am the yoga mistress. The ear mistress will have decided to shut down. She is the composer of the music you have been listening to and has detected a change, maybe a new instrument in the arrangement.'

A face appears and like an orange panther she is in the tunnel stalking her prey. Contorting herself around the machine, she uses her bodily strength to free something. The machine is restarted and the sound feels physical after the silence. The shift end is the reverse of the start, the sound diminishes and now the lift strives for the surface. I ask why they volunteered for this work.

My guide replies, 'you will see,' and I do. The world has changed, or maybe I have. The blackness is many shades of grey and the sky is, well, beautiful sky. 'Come and have a shower'. They had arrived as women. Down below they were 'other' and now, shiny and wet, they are girls. My intuition tells me I will have to rewrite my story since love, underground, may be a hindrance.

Eleanor is watching me, she is a few years older than I but far younger than the rest of the group. She asks, 'what do you see?'

'Girls,' I reply, thoughts are unfiltered when you are naked and wet.

'Then you will be welcome.'

I feel like one of the flowers, when we are leaving for home. I am staying with Eleanor; am I intruding when she embraces her partner? I do not want to burst their bubble of love. She introduces me in the strangest way. 'Angela, this is Susan, the reason I told you to put your imagination away.'

Susan looks at me with an inner smile, 'so you fell in love her as well. Dinner is ready.' We eat contentedly in silence. Susan opens some strawberry wine to lubricate our conversation afterwards and opens with, 'she can read minds, they all can, it comes with the job. I can read her and she likes you, so tell us, honestly, why are you here.'

'You don't believe I'm here to write a radio play set in your world?'

'You must be desperate for ideas.'

Honesty is the best glue, and they obviously have it in abundance. 'I really am going to write, but there is a reason. In the Office of National Information there is a woman who understands numbers; today I saw what she sees. In a few years Eleanor will be alone underground. I have to write a story which would encourage even me to be a miner. I was planning to write a love story, but I now see that is all above ground.'

'But, you know why that is,' Eleanor suggests, 'you saw how beautiful the world is when you emerged.'

'And, I'm obviously more attractive than a coal face,' Susan concludes. 'Actually, all the partners of the women you saw would say the same.'

Eleanor prompts me, 'what did you see?'

'You mean – girls. Most of us have two or three good

friends, but you all have each other.'

'Except in my case I have a dozen mothers,' she says ruefully. 'I have everything I ever wanted, but seeing you down there made me want more. Write your story so I can be like the others in thirty years from now.'

'You should go tonight,' Susan says and then to me, 'there is a social club, no partners, underground only, so you qualify. It will be good research and good fun.'

The evening is cold and dark; walking to the club is similar to riding to the coalface. There are sounds which become more distinct as we approach. A door opens and a shaft of light becomes sound; just as lightning precedes thunder. We are still some distance away when the door closes. The last fragments of sound float past; made distinct by the darkness. They give a vision of what is happening inside; a laugh; an exclamation; a clattering of skittles. The portal opens for us and we are part of it.

Our presence is acknowledged on the edge of perception. There are league tables for every kind of game around the walls, which let you know how active the club is. Eleanor is a rare visitor and her name is at the bottom of most of these; this dubious honour is shared with another Angela who is obviously equally as absent. Two women approach us.

'Hello mum,' are Eleanor's first words.

The other woman then says to me, 'you took my daughter's advice, I'm glad you came; we all really want to know why you are here.'

Eleanor sums up my quest, 'she's going to find me a group of friends.' Another woman has gravitated towards us and those last words has brought her into orbit. In the spirit of the place I say.

'I didn't recognise you with your clothes on, you are the chief girl.' I am referring to the pranks I had seen in the shower. Her reply will be in my radio play.

'Thank you, I've been chief girl for fifty years; it's why I haven't retired yet. Do you know we get paid for enjoying ourselves like that? I've come to take Eleanor away, she needs to set a new record.' As she is led away it is left to Susan's mum to explain.

'Eleanor holds the record for the most kilowatts in five minutes, that is how we power the club.' I can see that quite a crowd has gathered around the cycle generator and they give a lot of encouragement. A pink Eleanor returns; not her best but still better than anyone else in the last twelve months. Watching the nature of the compliments she receives, on her way back to us, I decide I had better do some serious research.

'I see what you mean about the mothers; I've met the chief girl and you are the chief child. If I'm going to save you I will need a love story.' Eleanor's mum then writes my play.

'We all fall in love, especially underground. There have been no serious accidents for a long time but we have the rule that only one of a partnership can work there. Susan sacrificed what you saw today to be with Eleanor. There is an even greater love,' she looks at Susan's mum, 'not asking for the sacrifice.'

I do not know, yet, how I can turn that look into sound but I think I ought to ask, 'may I use your story? You don't have to tell me what happened, I can imagine.' I am remembering when Eleanor had wiped my lips, in any other context it would have been an act of love. Maybe she is now reading my thoughts.

'You won't recognise yourselves and I won't tell any of your friends.' To me she says, 'and now it's your turn to be everyone's daughter, come on.' She leads me to the cycle; I can ride a long way but not very fast. As I start to pedal, she announced to those who had come to watch. 'We have a new competition; the most kilowatts in an evening. Angela is going for a leisurely ride; to keep her going you have to come and tell her why you enjoy being a miner.' I find out many things and none of them are negative.

They are indeed paid for the time in the shower and for the long summer holidays when coal is not needed. There are just as many jobs above ground; Susan and Eleanor's situation is quite common and their relationships are as strong as the one I have seen. Every woman there has two hearts; one for a partner and one for their friends. They are unaware how special their situation was. I cycle for over an hour and generate nearly five times what Eleanor had done in five minutes; I am at the head of a new table. The scenery has been amazing on my ride.

On the way back we link arms and Eleanor says, 'your partner will be very lucky when you find her.' When someone says something like that you have to ask why and she continues, 'you will imbue every act with meaning, so she will feel loved; just teach her to bubble her tea.'

## Freda – The Interview

When I was growing up Freda was the physical Auntie; able to lift me at an age which could have been embarrassing but it actually removed a few years and I felt like a small child again. When I was interviewing her for my story I did not know what to expect.

The outdoor job she mostly did was thatching; she seemed to have tamed the sun in her face. Her hair was uncontrolled; bleached in such a way that she would never go grey; ageless. It all felt slightly formal. I was writing a story and she was a character in it. I started by telling her what Louise had said and the years just melted away.

'I remember those moments,' she said. 'The first time I saw her, yet another strange head in the bed next to mum. She did not seem surprised to see me and when she said, "I want to wake up next to that face for the rest of my life," mum just looked the happiest I had ever seen her. I didn't know that I had a veto on their happiness, children just see and say things as they are.'

'You know that neither I nor my story would exist if it wasn't for that moment.' I said, hoping it would move things along, and it did since she continued.

'That includes my story and Naomi's. I remember the day I saw forever. Louise was wondering how to complete her picture on the wind turbine; no-one wanted to ascend the inside to the top. "I need a chimney sweep," she had said and described how small boys would clean large chimneys hundreds of years ago. I volunteered and it was easy. You are climbing in the dark which makes the breakthrough at the top visually overpowering. I could see, if not forever, more than I had ever seen.'

There was another reminiscent pause. 'Louise said it was the first time you had called her Mama-Lou and it was that that made it so special.' I prompted.

'I understand that first Mama feeling now, back then it was just the obvious thing to say. I knew I would remember that day forever and she had created it.'

'How does Naomi fit into it?' I asked, Naomi had been my mentor for understanding life.

'She was my best friend, I couldn't leave her out of the most exciting thing that could happen to any nine year old. Louise explained that, although I could climb up, it was a far bigger task to paint the clouds. When she said that it made me want to do the job so much more. She drew a picture of all the things we would need to allow me to dangle safely fifty feet above the ground. There was even more just to get it there. Everything was correctly calculated but Louise was expecting it would go no further.'

'It became Naomi's adventure to find all the things we needed; then it became a class adventure to build the prototype. Older girls were jealous that we were having so much fun at school. Mainly because the design was for a small girl like me so they could not play on it. All my friends did but not way up in the air, like me. Naomi did the ascent to help me assemble it but she wasn't as happy as I was. She is the first one to call me "Freda the Fearless."'

'Was there anything else you remember from that time?' I asked and was surprised by how serious she looked.

'When I was ascending, in the dark, I thought about the chimney sweeps, they were boys. In darkness like that you cease to exist when you cannot see your limbs. I had the strange feeling that I could be a boy.'

'But we don't know what it is like to be a boy.' I remonstrated, 'certainly not one from the past.'

'I know,' she said, 'that is why I'm glad to be alive today. There is something in me which would have been unhappy in the past. Not allowed to be the person I really am.'

'So who is that?' I asked.

After some reflection she said, 'I didn't know until you

just asked me to put it into words. I am the one who could say "I did that." I never do when someone is admiring my work. The light on the spire is the best thing I ever did and I was only fourteen.'

I was surprised by this revelation, it had been a mystery for over thirty years. 'You can't stop there!' I blurted out.

'And you mustn't tell anyone until I retire. You know the story; there used to be a light when there were aeroplanes. It was almost as much a symbol as the spire itself. Like many things it fell into disuse. Louise told the story and made changing the bulb sound like an epic adventure. It was Naomi's idea; she found an old road sign powered by a windmill. With this and an adapted bedside light she created the "beacon". It may need replacing soon.'

'When I was climbing inside the spire I was surrounded by centuries of creativity. It is quite humbling and made me want to make something which lived beyond me. I also knew I was a woman when surrounded by structures of men.'

I was speechless. Freda and Naomi had created an icon. Young children are admonished, 'if the beacon doesn't light you will be sorry you wasted that!' At school we were taught the relationship between how alight the beacon was and the supply of electricity and water. Tourists just marvelled when they saw it beaming in the darkness.

I could see Freda's eyes twinkling as she read my thoughts. 'That's right,' she said, 'every time someone is talking about it I feel fit to burst to tell them. I resist the urge so the feeling spreads all the way to my toes and I am walking on air.'

'If you could read my thoughts now, you would probably float away,' was all I could think to say. Details of the rest of our meeting are mostly in my story. I promised to keep her secret until she was ready to float away. That is the end of my eulogy. In memory of Freda I think we should make sure the beacon does not die with her.

# Olaf's Big Adventure

I could have walked, but it was raining, which is why I was in my car. I know it is wasteful but our evening roast was well advanced and we needed Yorkshire Puddings, so I did have two reasons. My car is called Olaf because he is small, white and friendly; that is to the environment, electric with a sixty mile range. By the way, I did succeed, but I ate the evidence. I should have been driving faster, but charity and not running over your neighbours begins at home. So I did not, run her over. My avoidance looked like I had intended to park more neatly than I usually do.

You know how modern cars lock the doors when you set off, and stay locked when you stop? She could not get in. She was frantic, and then in despair; she saw me pressing the wrong button to unlock the doors. She was desperate but her look of despair was the one she reserved for muppets. I found the symbol with an open lock and she was in the passenger seat before I could turn back. I was surprised by her alacrity and then by her gun.

'Drive!'
'Where?'
'Anywhere!'

Mirror, signal, manoeuvre. I had only done the first bit when I told her, 'there are two men running this way. Are they anything to do with you?' Unexpectedly, she pulled off her hair. Suddenly blonde, she leant over and gave me a passionate kiss. On rainy days my car steams up quickly, clearing it reduces your range. I thought I should tell her that we would not get very far if she carried on. I kept this to myself as the gun was still between us. I saw the men walking past, scanning the horizon. I knew not to attract their attention and, anyway, I did not want to kiss them. Disappointingly, she disengaged. I could taste her lipstick and saw my clownlike face in the mirror.

'Aren't you frightened?' She asked.

'Obviously! How am I going to explain this?' I replied pointing at my new decoration. Then I remembered the gun. 'Is it loaded? I'd hate to die accidentally, even in such a heart stopping embrace,' I have always used flattery in awkward situations.

'Just drive!' Not wanting to repeat our first conversation, I set off. My first stop was the local supermarket. 'What are you doing?' She asked incredulously, with her trigger finger twitching.

'I need to get something.' Her expression changed. She realised I had gained the upper hand. She could not force me to do anything in such a crowded place. Of course, I did not know I was such a master of subterfuge.

'Can you get me some wipes? I can't go anywhere looking like this, especially home.' She had an expression I have seen many times before. Exasperation. My husband does a very good one. It means I have won an argument when I was not even arguing.

'I'll need your card.'

'Sorry, I've only got these,' I said, holding up a couple of twenty pound notes.

Her eyes twinkled. 'That is perfect!' She gave me another brief kiss as she reached over for the car key. In a single movement she was out, leaving the gun on the seat. Am I that transparent? It was fully dark, now, so I felt inconspicuous enough to get out and plug the car in. She was back soon after, with very little change.

'Ok! Let's go,' this was said more as a command, than a thank you.

'Not yet, you have to wait until it has finished,' she could see I had not touched the gun. She had done everything gracefully up until now, but now she stomped off to the darkness at the edge of the car park.

The charging had stopped and I was wondering what to do, when a woman with a wet wipe smothered my face. 'Happy!

Now can we go?' I could tell that she was happy because I had not recognised her. I hesitated, I liked her more when she was happy and what I said next would change that.

'We can go, but only thirty miles.'

'Do you know how far it is to Cambridge?'

'One hundred and thirty miles, but I've always wanted to do that journey.' She looked at me as if I belonged to some parallel universe; I added optimistically, 'we could be there by lunchtime tomorrow.' All urgency had left her, like a spirit that had decided to walk because it would be faster. She waved her hand in a forward direction.

'Let's start your big adventure then.' As we passed the thirty signs leaving town we must have caught up with that spirit, 'does this car go any faster?' Quite logically I replied.

'Yes, but it will take longer.'

With an audible exhale, 'wake me up when we get there.'

'Does your gun have a safety catch?' I asked, using my one bit of knowledge of such things. There was no reply, except for a satisfying click. I was enjoying myself. Olaf did not usually have passengers; my husband got agitated at forty miles per hour on an open road. Thinking of him I wondered when he would realise I was not there. My guess was that, about now, cooking smells would begin to be slightly burnt smells, as the vegetables dried up. My name would be called out and maybe taken in vain; then what? The empty drive would eventually be noticed; that was a bone of contention because charging Olaf took priority. Two plus two equals four when you know the answer. Olaf's name would be cursed; he will have run out of electricity, no doubt.

I pulled into another supermarket for some free electricity. I got a thrill from the fact that she did not wake up. Olaf is so quiet and decelerates so gently; she only woke up when I got back in the car after connecting to the supply and spending some minutes wandering and wondering. She had the wild look of someone who should be in control but is not. That is a feeling I have experienced on all but the most sedate fairground rides.

I suppose my pointing the gun at her was contributing to her panic.

I gave her back the gun and she calmed down. Looking at her watch she said, 'one hundred and ten; that's why I need to retire; I'm getting too old for this,' a pause, an appraisal, 'where are we?'

'Charging. I reckon it will be an hour before we are missed. Sorry I lied before, we had more than thirty miles.'

'So after this charge we'll make it to Cambridge?' I smiled but she continued, 'be careful, men have died after they looked at me like that.'

Deflated, but not threatened, 'sorry, was I looking superior – I know something you don't.' She nodded. 'If you're my friend you'll understand it is not malicious. I always lose at those games where you have to keep secrets. I'm quite popular in the groups I inhabit; they call me the silent gossip.'

'So, what do you know that I don't?'

'After four quarter hours we'll have added twenty miles so we'll have fifty. That will be nearly halfway there from here.'

'Do we have to stop at every supermarket from here to Cambridge?'

'I have a friend on the way; we could stop and use the domestic charger; have a proper sleep.'

'You are insane!'

'My husband says that, just before he sees the light. Oh! First quarter finished, back in a minute.' I got out; disconnected; reconnected and resumed the conversation. Actually she was the one to pick up where we had left off; but a bit sarcastically, I thought.

'So what will you say, "long time no see. I'm travelling with an insane woman but don't upset her, she has a gun."' That's the one thing I cannot deal with because I would never do it myself. The hurt of sarcasm received showed on my face when I replied, 'I suppose that's what you thought five minutes ago.'

'Eh?' I saw her mouthing the words and then she exploded with laughter. 'That was brilliant, what job do you do?'

'I'm a librarian. I'm well known to all the important people in the town, that's why I needed the wet wipes.'

'Who are the important people?'

'Those who read books, obviously.'

She started laughing again, 'what will you tell the police when you get home?'

'The truth.'

'They won't believe you.' She was probably right, we sat in silence for a few minutes except for the occasional infectious sniggering. Another fifteen minutes were up, when I resumed my seat I started a new conversation.

'What job do you do?'

'I'm an assassin.'

'Is that an upmarket killer.' She smiled at that description so I continued, 'how do you get into that line of work?' No-one had asked that question before so the reply was slow and thoughtful.

'Family, my mother taught me. She retired when I came of age.'

'Retirement in your early fifties,' I mused wistfully, 'mine keeps disappearing over the horizon. I suppose the life expectancy could be low.'

'Forties! I was fifteen for my first solo kill. Twenty years is enough, I told them I wanted to retire.' Arithmetic is not my strongest ability unless you add the word years.

'You're not thirty-five, on a bad day you could pretend to be my daughter.' She was not impervious to flattery so I followed up with, 'what went wrong tonight?'

'I was setup,' she stopped and gave me the strangest look, 'how did you do that?'

'Do what?'

'You cracked me, I'm one of the best under interrogation.' We were silent for quite a while until I'd collected some thoughts.

'Two questions: why was my cash perfect and why did you leave the gun? I suppose you have a very low opinion of me.'

She studied me, 'look away. How would you have described me to the police?' I stared through the windscreen, trying to see her and there was nothing. Eventually I saw her lips, bright purple, and then her eyes delineated with something green and sparkling. I described this and she took one of the wipes and removed the only things I had recalled. 'So you see, if you had left me you would have described a non-existent woman. I had the cash to buy a new me before I disappeared. You are still here so I trust you enough to reveal myself.'

'I've read every kind of book; it's part of the job, recommending genres. I felt like I was in a romantic comedy, that was the best kiss I've ever had. We're in a thriller, tell me more and you may have to kill me.' I got out of the car, another fifteen minutes were up. This time I stayed out. I thought of all the characters, in my situation, that I had ever read about; it was sobering and I was not drunk. Then I counted the assassins who retired and got back in.

'You can't retire.' I said in conclusion, 'who do you think set you up?'

She was obviously thinking but said defensively, 'my mum retired!'

'But you were her pension. Sorry, I don't mean you were conceived solely for that reason.'

'She has been suggesting it would be nice to have a granddaughter.'

'Join the club! Five years of oblique questions and statements, "neither of you work from home much, this would make such a lovely nursery" or "I saw your friend Carol yesterday; I can't believe her little one is talking as well as walking." Dad doesn't help either, when I say we're trying he just says "that's the best bit." What does your mum say?' She shifted uneasily; a pretend stretch. They say nature abhors a vacuum; I often have the same relationship with silence; especially when I have a theme. 'I expect she says, "you were just what I always needed".'

'Stop!' She shouted, which made the following silence

stronger. It eventually imploded sending elements of her life story in all directions. 'You're right, tonight I was meant to be caught; sent to kill a dead man. They always promise to spring you, it engenders loyalty. Mum has been implying things I did not understand until now. I love her but I can't do what she did.' This last statement needed explanation.

'What can be so bad that an assassin thinks her mother has gone too far?'

'Dad was one of her targets; she also said I was lucky to be a girl.'

'What happens now?

'I really need to disappear.'

'Are we still going to Cambridge?'

'Maybe, but first we'll visit your friends neighbours.'

I saw the blue light in the mirror, another fifteen minutes were up. This time she got out with me. She looked nothing like the woman who had entered my life not so long ago. When I had reconnected the charger she said, 'come on, let's see what we can buy for two pounds ten pence.'

'Is that all that is left of the forty?' I did not hear the reply because she had sauntered off. I now realise she was sampling freedom. If she could succeed in disappearing this is what life would be like; not caring about cameras, she waved at the one in the entrance to the supermarket. Two pints of milk and a bag of crisps; we sat outside drinking the milk; she ate all the crisps.

Back in the car she seemed completely relaxed, I thought she would make a very good friend. 'Let's go, tell me when you have ten miles left.' How can she look so innocent when she's asleep. I can have a sleepless night when one book is found on the wrong shelf. I was excited for Olaf; he had never been this far before. I hoped she had a plan as the low charge indicator started to flash; it is very discreet in keeping with a car which purrs. I pulled into a pub car park and stroked her leg to wake her. She blinked awake and said with a yawn, 'would you like a job as my chauffeuse? What time do you think it is?'

'About ten thirty, why?'

'That's a good time to go for a walk.'

It was a village with sporadic street lighting. I was suddenly alone and a dog was barking in a nearby house. 'Not that one,' she said suddenly reappearing. How had I been transformed into a burglar in such a short time? She found what she wanted, waiting until no cars were passing before slipping in. I followed; I felt so clumsy tripping over things which she intuitively avoided. I was admonished.

'Wait here, don't move.' It reminded me of childhood, I was not invited on all the fun things. She appeared at the front door and waved me in. As she talked I realised I had missed the excitement again. 'I found one of those narrow windows openable, so I slithered in. I've turned the wifi off so the camera on the doorbell won't report us. They are on holiday for another week, according to their family planner. I'll cook us a feast while you get the car.'

'You're assuming I won't run away.'

'Yes.'

'I'll be an accomplice if I don't raise the alarm.'

'You have a defence, in that case,' she looked at me menacingly, 'I know where you live!' Her stare turned into a grin. 'You are not an accomplice, you are my best friend. When you return, park right at the back so I can turn the wifi on.' I was getting used to my role; I remembered to close the gates once I had driven in; the all-seeing bell would report nothing untoward.

I realised I was hungry when I entered the kitchen to the smell of steak grilling; so I contributed Yorkshire Puddings to the feast. 'Nice place you have here,' I said, 'very kind of you to invite me to dinner and charge my car.'

'Will you be staying long?'

'At least six hours.'

'In that case I'll make up a bed for you.'

'That's very kind.'

'It's what best friends are for, cheers.'

'Let's talk when we have eaten,' I said, 'you're making me

laugh too much.' While she washed up, I surveyed the bedrooms; I felt like Goldilocks. Seriously, the main bedroom had a large double bed with a hard and soft side. When she came up she found me asleep in baby bear's bed.

She whispered softly, 'someone has been sleeping in my bed, and she's still here!' When I looked semi-conscious, 'it's time for you to go.'

'What? Have I?'

'Yes, the full six hours, I've been thinking; you can go home. Don't look so sad, my life is going to become very dangerous.'

I've had a best friend for a few hours and slept through most of it was my main thought, 'what will you do?'

'I may never be safe, but there are a few men,' she paused, 'to eliminate first.'

'Is it revenge?'

'Partly, but they want to do the same to me.'

'I thought you were going to disappear.'

'I already have, thank you for your help in that. The problem is when I strike they will know it is me.'

'Then hire someone else to do it.' She smiled at my naivety and I felt it. It was never like this in the books I read. Then she made me feel very special.

'Tell me what you would do.'

I started foolishly, 'I would become a super-assassin.' She would have smiled again but I ploughed on, 'adopt a persona, you could be like me, the librarian. Kill them in interesting ways that you have found in books. Leave the passage with their body.' She gave me such a hug I could hardly breathe. She noticed and stopped; we did not say anything else. I started homeward; she kept the gun but gave me the assassin suit and wig. I left a note on baby bear's bed from Goldilocks.

I had been missed but not reported missing; neither had a murder been reported in the area. I never asked my husband what he thought had happened and he never asked. I was now a mysterious woman and more attractive because of it. When I wore the assassin suit and wig I became an incredible kisser. I had it dry-cleaned recently because it will not fit for a while now. My mum was pleased with the news and my dad said, 'it's not an excuse to give up trying.'

Pre-natal maternity leave is the New Forest of time. Normal life flies by in small fields allotted to specific activities. Now, with four weeks and nothing to do, time feels like a vast plain with no boundaries. The New Forest is my chosen metaphor because I do not contemplate anything longer. What did my mother do before the internet.

It is a year since my and Olaf's big adventure. I search for the news in Cambridge a year ago. It is fascinating, I am confident that she was involved and that she was not caught. I wonder if she took my advice. There are many links to follow, any mystery is fertile ground for outlandish theories; when you know a little of the truth they are all merely entertainment.

I was wanting my waters to break to stop me going down these interminable rabbit holes. I came across a post from 'bibliotecaria'. She suggested a better story to look at. I was getting excited for the first time in weeks, the news item linked to flashed onto my screen and my waters did break.

# April Shower

'April Shower! Is that your real name?' She asks this with an inflection of disbelief. Here they are; three highly paid television news producers to interview a drama school graduate for the job of weather presenter.

'Of course not.' Is the candid answer. The man on her left, almost imperceptibly, starts to pay attention. The skill he has, which has elevated him to his current position, is an air of boredom which makes people try harder to impress him. This time he has difficulty maintaining his affectation. Her reply has been the perfect balance between admitting guilt but leaving the questioner wondering why they have asked.

'Then why?' He asks this hoping to upset that balance. The answer feels like a safety net which he has unwittingly tumbled into.

'It got me into this seat, didn't it?' Both interviewers are now quiet because they cannot ask their prepared follow up questions. The third interviewer has more important things to do and is not even listening. She is the one in charge.

'Sorry, the one o'clock news will need me. I'll leave one question. Do you think a weather presenter should have studied meteorology?' Does she have a third eye for navigating? Her gaze is firmly fixed on her tablet as she leaves hastily; negotiating the room's obstacles like a premier league footballer about to score the goal of the season. From the corridor there is a shriek; some inanimate object will be getting a red card.

In the interview room a unanimous decision is needed; which never happens with these two. There is no breaking news; the woman who has left has already chosen who will get the job. She will ask, 'did you find someone?' Expecting the answer, 'no'. April's answer, to the question left hanging, secures her the job.

'There is a script isn't there? I'm not sure I could ad lib. I have friends who can but I'm just not very good at it.' She pauses but is met by silence. She realises she has to say more. 'You know, you had me there; thinking the forecast is made up on the spur of the moment. If someone else writes the words, I can deliver them.'

The woman knows that the colleague who had posed the question would have been merciless. The poor girl would wish she had never applied. Actually, someone else does write the words and she is sure the delivery would be good. After all she has been on the receiving end of it. Showing no emotion she says, 'can you wait outside for a moment.'

When they were alone she asks the man, 'have you got some real work to do?'

'Obviously!' He replies. 'You know we won't agree and be overruled.'

The woman can see past the man's insouciance. 'I can tell you would welcome her into your home every night.'

He giggles. 'Don't tell my husband – he might change channel to annoy me.'

She conspires. 'For once I agree with you. She will be the cherry squidged in the icing on the bun of news. It is the only bit most people are interested in.'

'So what are you suggesting?'

'Give her the job. Send the rest away so that you don't have to look, and I don't have to be, bored all morning.'

April is astounded by her success. It had been the suggestion of her tutor. 'You don't need an acting job to act. Apply for any old job and treat the interview as an audition.' Using silly names had worked in getting more interviews than real applicants could hope for. Surprised, but not overcome, she quickly registers 'April Shower' as her stage name. She is sure she could get parts in pantomime if things do not work out.

April becomes the woman everyone invites into their home. She makes the weather interesting and she finds that she can ad lib. All three interviewers will often say how they saw her potential and argued that she should have the job. A fourth person to benefit from association was the intern who had put

April on the shortlist; she will mention this to any man she fancies. Her line is, 'the last person to make my shortlist was April Shower.' Why this works as an enticement can only be imagined.

April really does have magical powers. For over ten years she is the last person most people remember before going to bed. The love for her only increases when she becomes pregnant. When your baby first kicks it is a surprising but joyful moment. This happens to April with millions watching just as she says, 'high pressure is dominating so there will be no surprises for a few days.'

By late June she is heavily pregnant and has the following exchange with the newscaster before her forecast. He asks, 'we are all wondering when your last forecast will be.'

'You know the people of Cornwall have asked me to stand further west so they can see their county. The problem is the weather.' She pauses long enough to gain the viewer's attention. 'This warm spell makes my bump fidgety; so to come to an air-conditioned studio is bliss.'

The news reader concurs. 'It seems working from home is less popular when the temperature gets above thirty.' This must have been rehearsed because April shows a map of the Shetland Isles.

'This is the place to be; a pleasant twenty degrees; the size of Greater London with a fraction of the people; at this time of year it does not actually get dark.' This is forgotten by everyone except one person in the following month.

The forecasts during her tenure had become amazingly accurate. This was a combination of computing power and what was called AI. It was only the ability to compare historical weather charts with the current situation but it was an important refinement. In her last forecast before maternity leave she does the kind of ad lib for which she was famous. 'In summary, it is a bucket and spade day on the south coast tomorrow. Further north your time will come.'

It could have been a tragedy when a waterspout comes

ashore the following day. In the mayhem of flying buckets and spades a young girl is cut by a fold-up chair hurled in her direction. Her mother posts a video in praise of the beach medics who treat her. It concludes with a close up of the girl with a bandage round her head and the words, 'of course we were only here because April suggested it.'

April is unaware of this because her labour starts when the studio lights go down. There is not much news in the summer so April and her baby get as much attention as royalty. She did not help matters by being so nice about what is really intrusion. When your sleeping, at last, baby is woken by photographers you should not say, 'I expect he'd like to get back inside me, away from all of this.' You certainly should not smile, it only encourages them.

April has just seen herself saying, 'away from all of this,' on the happy part of the news. Her husband slumps down beside her, cradling a peaceful baby with a clean nappy.

'There's still someone outside,' he says glumly. 'I expect they are going to record when the lights go on and off.'

April looks at her son and asks him. 'Do you want us to keep all the best wishes cards so that you can play with them when you are older?'

'That's another thing! How am I going to sneak out to the recycling with them all? Any more and we'll have to move.' This is said by a man who loves his wife and his son. It makes these minor annoyances bearable. The piles of cards are a socio-economic investigation waiting to happen. The conclusion will be that all levels of society, and locations, love April. She is fingering one of the cards.

'We have dozens like that. I suppose there is a limited choice at short notice.' He makes this observation which any human would. Somewhere in a warm, dark and dry facility an AI program is calculating to the wrong conclusion. A client company making baby equipment will overproduce with financial consequences. The next card she handles is hand-made.

'We won't recycle this one.' There is a picture of a cot with a mobile over it and the caption, 'pre-loved by one careful owner.' Inside is a picture of a girl, uncertainly standing and underneath, 'my first word was April and my second was Shower.' A message is on the facing page. 'It does get pretty lonely here and there are no disposable nappies. If you need time away she is your number one fan.'

Two days later they decide to take up the offer. The TV company are happy to help with a bit of subterfuge. Their job is to report the news not be it. No-one asks where they plan to go when they are dropped off at King's Cross station one morning. Everyone thinks they know what April looks like, but that is the woman with shoulder length hair and studio make-up not the bleary-eyed mother with hair in a bun. No passengers on the train to Aberdeen or the overnight ferry to Lerwick give her a second glance; in fact most avert their gaze when she is breast-feeding.

Meanwhile on another continent a man with a theory is looking for proof. The weather forecast is never wrong but that is because it is a plan – devised by a government weather controller. It is not going well; he decides that they will obviously hide how they do the big events so he looks for something smaller. Living where he does, which has more climate than weather he is unfamiliar with many terms. He does not know why he goggles 'april shower'.

Somewhere in the recesses of his mind his grandmother had said something which her grandmother had said when describing the old country they had come from. It is important that a voice in his head is guiding him when the first page is filled by one woman. A weather presenter who knows nothing about the weather and is named after a phenomenon. She disappears after one bad forecast. Obviously she was not sticking to the script and had to go.

He delves further; the video clip of baby's first kick was clearly when she had received her first warning; the clip of the girl with the bandaged head showed she was becoming more powerful than the controllers; now she has disappeared! He posts these thoughts in a place they will be well received and then forgotten about.

News organisations cannot be everywhere. When the story of April's baby began to fill a void they all needed something for their websites. One company saved some money by using AI to merge available pictures and claimed the result was their own. They did not know about the watermark added by the program owners. Actually it was not AI but just a clever program; however they could charge more by branding it as AI.

It was the best picture available and so was syndicated. Foreign websites found the story amusingly British. 'Not only are they renowned for talking about the weather but now they have a Queen of it.' It should have been a short-lived scandal; who really cared? Or rather what really cared? This was the actual problem. There was a bot designed to look for stolen images.

When you want a royalty payment why not go for maximum publicity. The headline was '99% of images of April Shower and her baby are fake!' Ignoring the fact that it was one image on over a thousand sites. This story breathes life into the post by the conspiracy theorist but it will still die soon enough.

Who pays for the sites which host outlandish ideas. It will be obvious when I tell you. To develop an AI you raid everything on the internet except the obviously deluded. That means you have to know where it is and be able to control it. Finally you realise what a good test resource it is; you feed it to your AI and hope that it is rejected.

The trouble with computer programs is that they are their most interesting when they go wrong. If your job is limited to testing them then that is the greatest excitement. The text of the email was.

*We have a problem unless it is true*

*Weather presenter silenced by controllers! Where is April Shower?*

The content was a test run of a particular version; the

hacker with the job of infiltrating a rival company only extracted these sentences; English was not his first language. A quick search found the article about fake pictures so he posted the question.

*Where is April Shower? Did she ever exist?*

The science of tricking an AI into spiralling destructive feedback had not been established but it had to start somewhere.

April's son was only two weeks old when the police broke into their house to find the lights all controlled by timers. They were forced to do this by the media circus camped outside. They then had to make a show of questioning the TV company executives. The internet did not believe, 'helping them get away for some peace and quiet.'

If April had posted a 'here I am' video it would not have been believed because of all the fake ones available. The mother of the daughter with the bandage was offered a considerable amount of money if she would let her girl make a video asking April to come home. Sensibly she refused but someone created one anyway. This effort was rewarded by many likes so that every celebrity posted one, real or fake.

There were so many threads to this story that you could weave a tapestry. There were earnest debates on the right to privacy. April was becoming the figurehead of a movement which would undo thirty years of technological advance. How had she achieved this? There is no secrecy as we return to the Shetland Isles early one morning.

An eighteen month old girl runs towards our travellers. 'April Shower! April Shower!' She calls.

A bystander asks, 'when's your girl going to learn more words?'

Her mother catches up and introduces them. 'Hi I'm Isla and this is Freya.'

April responded, 'I'm Olivia with Ben and baby. He came a bit sooner than expected so he can wait a bit longer for a name.' To Freya she says, 'I'm glad you recognised me. I was beginning to wonder if I was still me.'

Isla is surprised at how little luggage they have. 'You're taking me at my word that I'll have everything you need.'

April really is the woman you would invite into your home. 'One day when you visit London I will reciprocate. Actually I have brought everything which currently fits and Ben would be stitched into his clothes if it was still the fashion.'

They live a few miles out. Ben is in the back squashed between two child seats. Freya shows she understands far more language, after a little thought she says, 'baby Shower.' Everyone laughs in a way that tells her she made the correct deduction.

When they arrive Isla knows there is no point talking. Even friends who live nearby are speechless at the view. This time she does have something appropriate to say. 'As you can see we don't really need your forecasts. We can see the weather coming.' She only has to explain one thing because everything else is obvious. 'The TV set is not broken. I never watch it when my husband Tom is away. With no internet the rest of the world does not exist.'

Ben asks in the nicest way. 'That must make you special but I can't imagine how.'

He gets a glimpse of happiness when she replies. 'He works on the oil rigs; four on; four off. When he comes home I get all the news but filtered through him. That is still more than enough and he teases me with it.'

There is nothing interesting for an outsider to say about a baby. For the parents everything is noteworthy and important. Ben has new respect for his grandmother living in a world before disposable nappies. With no distractions they have time for other things. The French for boardgame is jeu de societe which is a far better description.

One morning Ben is transporting a nappy. He can navigate to the bucket in his sleep, if necessary. On the way back he sees a vision. Isla is wearing a smock dress over her jeans and has let her hair down. She is pleased by his expression. 'Tom will be home today,' she explains.

'Lucky Tom!' Is all he can think to say before he hurries

back upstairs.

A little later they are sat at the table after another leisurely breakfast. Olivia remarks, 'I think baby has adapted well to this lifestyle. Feeding him on the tube would be a shock for both of us.'

'So you're going back to work then?'

'Not immediately but going anywhere involves becoming a mole. Hmm I see - tell everyone to visit me.'

Isla sees Ben's expression and comments. 'Ben is alarmed by that.

'He overthinks things. Right now he is wondering if you are a Norse Goddess.

Isla has the perfect reply. 'The reason why Freya first said "April Shower" is that you are a goddess; at least to Tom and his friends.' On cue Tom arrives home and Freya rushes to him.

'Daddy, April Shower.'

Tom swings her up and says to her nose. 'I'll have to teach you some more words.'

She replies. 'No! Daddy! Look! April Shower here,' and she points to the kitchen table.

Now he would be lost for words in this situation regardless of the furore surrounding April. They are not expecting what he finally says. 'What... How... You melted the internet.' The tone of what follows is set by Isla's comment.

'You see, whatever has happened Tom makes it more interesting.' She got up to make Tom's favourite breakfast and Olivia follows whispering.

'What would you be doing now if we weren't here?

Isla smiles and says. 'Not this, but something big has happened and his mind would not be on it anyway.' Olivia realised that Isla would be her best friend from now on and said.

'First we'll let him tell us, his way, to get it out of his system and then we'll take Freya for a long walk.'

Ben had selected a game of Cluedo to play. He suggests that playing and talking at the same time may help, 'because melting the internet will be difficult to explain.' While they are setting up Tom asks.

'What's the baby's name?'

'We haven't done that yet, no rush, you have six weeks.'

Tom grins. 'You have no idea,' but does not elaborate. He does some calculations. 'I will still be here when the six weeks are up. We will have to smuggle you somewhere.'

Nothing more was said except. 'Professor Plum in the Library with the Lead Pipe.' Isla finally broke.

'Tom I know you love playing this game.' Which has two meanings in this context. 'But you have got to explain what has happened.'

'The whole world is playing Cluedo. It all went berserk when they realised you hadn't registered the baby's name. You have been seen in every corner of the planet.'

Ben objects. 'The world is spherical, it doesn't have corners.'

'Exactly.' Tom replies and realises that Ben could be a best friend. At this point baby disrupts the game. Freya stares intently as Olivia starts to feed him but then goes back to arranging some bricks. Tom also watches and then looks to his wife; she understands his thoughts and does not say no or yes with her eyes. Maybe I should find a local job first he thinks which is why, a propos of nothing he asks.

'What job do you do Ben? It seems to let you take time out.'

'Script consultant. Well, that is what I tell those who work in the media. They usually lose interest when I say that.'

Olivia butts in. 'Ben is far more important, he is a meteorological modeller. His computer programs inform my scripts. That is how we met.'

Ben continues. 'Actually I've already taken too much time out. I only booked the paternity leave allowance so they will be wondering where I am.'

Tom is thinking and smiling. 'This is going to be fun. You have no idea what will happen if you suddenly reappear. We'll have to make them work to figure it out. Tomorrow we will register your baby's name. If they ask, you are my old friend from university who arranged the holiday and didn't want an early arrival to stop it.'

Isla joins in. 'I've been watching you, staring at the view. You can tell your work you are on location formulating a new model.'

Ben decides she must be Norse Goddess. 'How did you know?' He asks.

In the real world people have friends they can trust. Ben's email is forwarded from an oil rig in the North Sea. It is three days before a television crew in a helicopter is asking for permission to land. It takes a week for the registration to filter through and be recognised for what it is. Interest is waning; there is now some more important news and the internet has regained its composure. Some journalists make a few telephone enquiries because they baulk at the time needed on the ferry.

One week later Isla's phone rings. 'Is Ben available?' A voice enquires. The caller must know that Ben is there.

Isla manages to ask, 'who...' but is interrupted.

'Is calling? Tell him an irate sister.'

'You don't sound irate. He's outside looking at the view, will Olivia do?'

'Put me on loud speaker so you can all hear when you've retrieved Ben.'

When they have all assembled Isla asks. 'Ben wonders which irate sister it is.'

'The pregnant one who has been visiting their house to look after it. You all owe me the biggest of favours. I knew where you were from the beginning. I tidied away your lovely card before anyone noticed it. I'm calling to let you know it is now safe to come back. Please don't look at what has been happening; especially when I turned up at your house in the dress you lent me. I reckon a lifetime of Christmas and birthday presents will not be enough. Mum thinks you did it on purpose so that she couldn't interfere – not her actual words.' Everyone laughs and Isla takes the phone outside.

'I'm going to take some pictures and send them to you. You can have the same offer as Olivia. I think Ben is a better father because of the experience.'

The story does not end when they return unnoticed to their home, but a lifelong friendship does not make interesting reading. Olivia gave a short interview to explain that April Shower would not return because she wanted to explore her first love, acting.

The man with a theory to prove added his final post on the subject after watching the interview many times. *April Shower did not exist and now she has been deleted.*

# Stonehenge Scaffolding

It is sad being the last. No-one believes my stories. They would like to but they are wedded to the times we live in. They think it is the beer talking. They think they have to buy me a drink to get me started. They never tire of my opening phrases. 'I am the last of a long line of scaffolders. Longer than that of the kings and queens of England and Spain combined.'

It all started when Stonehenge was assembled. I have no idea how they did it but clearly they would have some scaffold. One of the prompts they use on me is. 'Tell us about the birds'. They are referring to the Great Bustard which has been reintroduced to the Plain. The first time someone mentioned it is when I became, 'The Old Man in Residence,' at my local pub. The annoying thing is that I don't think I'm old.

'They'll be sorry,' I said, 'it's the reason that Stonehenge Scaffolding became a permanent operation. They're tasty birds but Great in name and Great in pooping. Cleaning those stones was a seasonal activity.' If they buy me three drinks I'll sing the them the 'approach song'. You can't just stick up your scaffold without asking permission, after all.

Tonight I am sat in the corner with my great-niece Alice. She affords me some protection from those who would ridicule my tales. When she was small, afore she went to school, I told her my stories and she believed me. Her head is so full of the sense that they force into their ears that she has lost her sense of wonder.

She went to the stones last week for the rite of passage. Those lucky enough to have finished their exams go to watch the solstice sunrise. Many are watching the sun rise on their own life. 'Are you going straight to university?' I ask. I like her reply.

'I have to. I have this feeling that, if I find anything better to do, I will lose the urge.' I interpret this as somewhere inside her she knows there is more to life than what is on the standard map. Her next question confirms this. She wants to know what my map looked like.

'Why did you never marry? Grandma says every girl would have said yes.'

'It doesn't work like that, all the young men in this bar and all the others would say "yes" to you, if you asked.'

'I'm nowhere near ready for that!'

'Exactly, the stars have to align. You see Tom over there; he's waiting for the girl of his dreams. He'll know her when he sees her but she has to see him too. He's worked with us since he left school. I like him because he doesn't make fun of me like all the others.' I cannot talk quietly so Tom hears his name. When he catches Alice looking at him intently he decides to come over.

'My ears were burning, what has he been telling you?' Alice is very diplomatic.

'He likes you, you must be a good scaffolder.'

'Has he been telling you how to catch a man.'

Alice gives me a quizzical look and says slowly. 'No'

'Oh.' Tom is deflated but recovers. 'I thought he might be telling you about the "love stones".' I'm sure Tom wants to believe because he speaks matter of factly. This encourages me to explain.

'You were asking why I never married. If you find your one true love you never grow old in their eyes. But how can you be sure?' I pause to allow Alice time to make connections.

'So when grandma says, "every girl would say yes", you needed some other confirmation.'

'All you have to do is squeeze between the "love stones" and look into each other's eyes.

I think Tom is more romantic than Alice who is looking very sceptical, with a slight sigh he says.

'That sounds a lot easier than studying profiles and going on dates; pretending to be interested in things you've never noticed before.'

Alice is concerned. 'Can it happen by accident? I'm pretty sure I was squeezed with someone at some point last week. The solstice is like a football crowd.'

I put her mind at rest. 'Of course not. You have to sing the songs. One sings the approach song and the other the love song. That is why I never had the chance; when I was Tom's age the stones were a "no go" area.' Tom makes a comment whose meaning depends on the way it is said.

'Do you think it would be an alternative to a diamond ring?' I think he really wants to believe.

I often visit Stonehenge, not spiritually but nostalgically for something which has been lost. 'I am going to the stones tomorrow morning. If you come along I'll point out the special stones to the pair of you.' Before he has chance to reply one of his friends comes over and puts a pint in front of me.

'Where's your manners Tom? Trying to get a story without paying for it. Tell us about the Romans, Jim!' Two others pull up a chair each. Alice has never seen this before and realises that Tom was actually being sympathetic compared to these friends. I start.

'You've heard it all before, but Alice hasn't for a very long time, so here goes. Being a Stonehenge Scaffolder was not a full time occupation. It was almost ceremonial, cleaning the stones before special events. Even the trees used to make the beams were special. It all changed when the Romans came. They were proper builders. Generations emigrated, their skills were needed all over the empire. There was always a kernel of believers in this area and they flourished again when first Old Sarum and then New Sarum were built. The best bit was they needed to scaffold to safely dismantle Old Sarum.'

Alice is watching the listeners and tries not to be indignant when she asks. 'Why do you do this?'

Tom answered. 'It makes us feel more important than the rest of the world thinks we are. We may not do what needs doing but they couldn't do it without us. We are there before the start and after the end.' The group lose interest when I refuse to sing a song. Tom is last to leave us and as he gets up to go Alice teases him.

'If you need an alibi. I'll be there tomorrow as well.' Alice is just eighteen and Tom is twenty-five but she causes him to blush; for more than one reason. The following day Tom is already there. We had only said morning and he didn't want to miss us; Alice mainly. I suppose she does look older; inheriting my sister's hair she already has some grey strands.

On the bus from the visitor centre there is a large and voluble Italian family. The only one keeping silent is the one I presume is the matriarch. There is a boy who can see us marvelling at the speed of the discourse. He is learning English at school and is brave enough to practice on us. 'This is grandma's birthday present. She was sixty this year. She has talked always of coming here. She has to do something.'

I don't think he understands my accent when I reply. 'Well we'll all be watching.' It is enough that he knows I understood him. The visit is a circular walk around the periphery. We take a long time. The Italian family fills the path and is moving very slowly; not by choice; the grandmother stops often and stares. When the circuit is complete they walk quickly to a waiting bus; except for the woman. She strides briskly to a particular spot and starts to sing.

Tom is the first to recognise it. 'That's your song with an Italian accent.' I walk around to where she is and confirm my suspicions. She is singing to the 'approach stones'. People are staring, especially her family. I do the only thing I can; I have to let her know that she is not alone. I start to sing the 'love song'. I realise how well the two harmonize. Of course she finishes first and considers me as my last phrases are solo. It seems natural that my last words are almost a whisper and also natural that I take her hand and lead her inside the circle.

Someone begins to follow to stop us but Tom calls out. 'Wait! They are falling in love.' I hear this and realise what I must do. I lead her to the 'love stones' and place her in between. It is designed for young lovers but, feeling only twenty years old, I squeeze in with her.

I look into the eyes of a beautiful young woman and in

the old language say. 'You are the one.' The spell is broken by the crowd calling to us to come out. The problem is that we are stuck. Even breathing in to speak is difficult. 'Why are they staying out there?' I ask not expecting a reply.

'Because only true lovers can enter the circle now.' She can feel my surprise because we are held so tightly together. 'I learnt English because I knew I would come here one day.' I decide that when we get out I will never accept beer for my stories again. I call to Tom and Alice to come and help and they do. Alice helps by smiling and Tom with instructions. The trick is to have our arms above our heads and move in opposite directions; a dance without music.

Her name is Alessandra and she directs Tom and Alice between the stones. 'I need to see how much weight he needs to lose.' When they are facing each other she says. 'Now relax and come out.' They are not stuck but they do have to coordinate their exit.

We leave the circle hand in hand. I wonder what we have done to Tom and Alice. I release her to her family and the boy gives us a translation. 'She says you were not stuck, you pretended and' slightly alarmed, 'she wants to be stuck to you forever, but grandad won't allow it.'

That was ten years ago and we keep in touch. I visit Italy at least twice a year. I now understand the effect of the stones. Her husband is retired now, as am I. He used to work in construction and we get on very well. Usually Alessandra translates for us but this time he took me aside to tell me via a translation App. 'I don't know how it works but when you come she is like the woman I married, and the effect lasts for a few weeks; so you're welcome any time.' He gives me a knowing grin and I raise a glass and say 'cheers'.

Alessandra appears at this point looking just like the woman he married and says to me. 'I'm sure you get younger every time you come.' That is the effect we acquired that day, nothing specifically to do with love. We see each other as we see ourselves. She was and is always twenty years old to herself.

When I look at her it strengthens her self-belief. In return she wills me to be younger. Not accepting beer for stories has helped.

I reply to her compliment in a way that only she will truly understand 'On that subject I have some news. Alice came home recently, she has a new job locally. Not many towns have careers for archaeologists. She has also given up the fight against grey hair which probably helps give her some gravitas at work. Tom was in the pub when we went for a drink. He is already balding I worry that he is following my lifepath. He came over and said, "you haven't changed a bit" and she replied "neither have you."' Then he just said, "so you'll marry me then," and without a thought she said, "yes."'

# Empty Room

He opened the door slowly, unsure what he was going to find. He hadn't been involved in the clearance. There was a slight smell of other, dormant odours disturbed. The outside world came faintly down the chimney, just the harmonics, nothing deep. He was barefoot to fully experience this last time.

The carpet at the entrance was worn hard and flat by a million footsteps. Where the rugs had lain he could feel the newness, softer to his curling toes. Around the edges, where furniture had left its mark, the indentations would need help to recover. The whole room was sighing with relief and the floor felt like a lawn recovering in Spring.

The silence was fragile. His steps echoed briefly as he displaced a loose floorboard. Even as he brushed his feet around the sound was alive. There it was, the coffee spill hidden by a souvenir from the bazaar in Istanbul. The stiffened pile caressed the arch of his foot.

The full, deadening, insulating curtains had been replaced by some rediscovered unlined ones. They had shrunk in the wash many years ago and now hung immodestly over the naked windows. He ran his hands down the freshly ironed material and found the tantalising gap above the window sill. The room seemed young and full of promise. The low winter sunshine warmed his ankles as he stood in the furthest corner. Would the new owners cause another fifty year eclipse.

He turned and with his peripheral vision saw the markings on the wall. The straight lines of the wall clock facing the curls of the mirror. They were flirting.

'I haven't seen you here before.'

'I've been here as long as you!'

'Well, now I've seen you, I don't want you to go.'

Their support screws were silent, they had seen it all before. Last time he had cut short the romance with a bold wallpaper. The ceiling was unobserved, the patchy repairs he had hidden in plain sight with matt white.

He left, firmly shutting the door. One million and one.

# Scales

Two hundred and eighty equal divisions on your ever darkening upturned face. Your sweeping arm so quick to reveal the truth with barely a quiver. All connected via a graceful neck to your sturdy floating platform, large enough for my feet.

In the past you looked too functional and so you gained some spare carpet, irremovably stuck. Wherever you are placed you leave an impression of your rectangular (slightly octagonal) base. Upside down you show your mechanism, but not how something so old and sturdy can be so precise.

Your measurements are in real units, a stone is something you can lift, a pound can be gained or lost in a natural human way or even just by flexing my foot, and so you force me to be still. I think you are your original colour, cream, when colour names were descriptive.

Because of my neglect you are now in need of a little Kurust. When I lift you, something knocks and you go negative, more weightless than an astronaut.

You have been around for my whole life and more, origin unknown. I remember when I made you jump to four and then more. When I came of age I was a sprightly ten, half of your maximum. Now I feel your reproach when fully clothed I reach twelve. So, barefoot to the neck, I ease your burden and my conscience.

When I peer down, not quite focussed, at where you have settled, I feel ageless. Half a century of metrication and digitisation disappears. You always tell me the truth of what I know already. As I write this, I am transported back sixty years into a bathroom with a plaster aquarium on the wall, but I cannot remember the floor. As the past becomes obscure I need to assure your future. Maybe, when my grandson can stand I will introduce him to you.

## The Colonists

'I've been experiencing your ideas on planetary tilt. You were thorough in your analysis. I don't pretend to follow all of your thoughts, but the gist is that a variation of about a quarter will produce the conditions for your evolutionary mayhem.' I signalled the affirmative; why was he taking such an interest? I had almost forgotten this thesis that I had put forward in my youth. I am still young, but we do live a very long time, and never forget; so I was ready for any difficult questions. His next thoughts surprised me.

'They've found one, and it is behaving oddly. My wife is organising the crew, I think you should join it.' He sensed my surprise. 'I know you have never thought to be a colonist, but if you are right your insights may be invaluable.' He waited for me to process the news. 'Good! When you are my age mind-reading comes naturally. Thank you for agreeing; two of your new colleagues will show you into the launch facility.'

Earlier today I had been preparing a lesson on planetary motion. Now I was sneaking into a spaceship; replacing someone who had been training months for the mission. We passed each other on my journey and he signalled 'thank you'; now that is worrying. She greeted me warmly, that slightly pink colour that suggests she likes me. I was a slightly brighter hue, she really is beautiful. I had many questions.

'Why am I here in one of the driving seats?'

'Someone has to sit there,' was the unhelpful reply.

'Doesn't it take a long time to master all these controls?'

She has such a lovely giggle, her tentacles undulating gently, as she informs me. 'It's all automatic, they control everything until we are in deep space.'

'But don't you spend ages training?'

Then she laughed, 'we have to pretend to learn. They don't realise we are far more intelligent than them; they think they designed all of this.'

'So what do we have to do?'

'We hibernate, it will be a very long journey. When we arrive we can override the automation, if we need to. They don't know that we know how to do that.'

'That makes it sound dangerous, is that why the swap was arranged? Was he scared?'

'No, he didn't like me!' I indicated that I could not believe that and she glowed perceptibly.

'But why does that matter?'

'You're innocence is so,' she paused, 'there is no word for a "window into a happy world". When we arrive we deploy the equipment as we have been trained; then we make love and colonise a planet.' We were all connected in a ring and I had to disconnect. This last thought rippled through the crew and was amplified on its passage. I had received the message directly and it stirred my feelings; the feedthrough was electric and I glowed bright red. She reconnected and gratefully absorbed my hormonal disturbance.

This really had been a last minute change. Lift off reminded me of being a child, playing in some hydrothermal vents. I know how evolution works but I can understand those who believe we were created for interstellar travel. Weightlessness is just the same as travelling in a perfect current. We can withstand high temperatures, perfect for a slingshot via the sun and re-entry. It is our ability to hibernate for thousands of years which is key to our success.

Just before we arrived our environment was warmed to gently end our slumbers. This was significant; generations could have passed at home but they were still watching us; even when a single message took twenty years to reach us. We became a shooting star over a planet which was two-thirds water. We landed with a splash which would have disconcerted the natives, if they had witnessed it.

'What happens now?' I enquired.

'We wait until the others have deployed their

experiments and then we swim off to discover this world.'

'When do we make love?'

'When we are far from the others.'

We loitered, examining our new home. Our jobs had been to sit in the driving seats, but no driving had been necessary. There was so much food, one stroke and the fish would wait obediently to be eaten. Eventually all the work was done and we all departed in our pairs. After a short time we could see red glows in the distance. 'This is far enough,' she imparted as she entwined our lower arms. 'I know you have never done this before, but I have.'

Each of her arms stroked and then wrapped around mine, pulling our bodies ever closer. When we touched our thoughts coalesced; we were of one mind; I felt as though I was ceasing to exist. Explosively we separated, left with each other's thoughts. I held her feeling, 'that was better than all the rest.' She looked at me, 'so, making love to me is even better than the existence of planetary tilt.' She was not mocking me, communication by thought has no barriers.

At the moment of ecstasy I had thought, 'who cares about planetary tilt, I want to be like this forever.' She knew that and instigated our union again. I left another thought with her, 'evolution stopped for us because any change would lessen this experience. Nothing could be better.'

'Wait until I invite you to my eggs,' was her reply.

We did wait. Planetary tilt causes migration. We hitched a ride on an enormous, air breathing, creature. She was travelling thousands of miles to a special place to have a child. Being present when she gave birth reminded us of our next task. We found an alcove and decided that it and the surrounding rocks would be a good nursery; some protection and there were plenty of fish. She was right about the act of fertilisation, for those moments we did not exist except as a beacon of pleasure. On return we were husband and wife, and all that that entails.

She swam into her hiding place and I directed fish there. Her womb grew until her arms could not surround it; then finally it broke free. I guided it to the spot we had chosen and then gradually let out our offspring over a wide area. We can hibernate but we do not need sleep, I did not stop; directing fish; imparting knowledge; most importantly nursing my wife back to health. This action is more intimate than making love; the tear from the womb needs to be sealed. Our bodies are private, but as a man my mouth can produce a sticky substance; using this I kiss my wife's wound away over a number of days.

Then we are both feeding our ever voracious young. Evolution is obvious, we must teach our children how to stroke fish, or we will all starve. They learn quickly, although it does not seem so, and they swim off to their destiny. The last lesson, how not to be another creatures meal, is the most difficult to teach. You have to let your children hurt you, until it really hurts. I love my wife, and so do they; she showed them the loving strokes; this means they do not want to hurt her!

That would be the end of our story: husband and wife; abundant planet; exploring and making love. My wife interrupts, 'that is your story, mine is wife and husband!'

One day, picnicking in a school of fish, we are hoisted from the water and dumped with the dying fish. We pacify as many as we can. These creatures are heartless, when I eat something at least it wants to be eaten. We are both lifted clear. Out of the water my wife is more nimble than I. She establishes communication with her captor with a delicate stroke of what I now know is an ear. Her message was simple,

'I taste terrible and prefer to be in the water.' It almost worked. I was squirming looking for some bodily contact past their fake skin. She does not blame me, just as we were about to be thrown back my captor called out and hers looked and thought 'only six'.

So here we are in a very pleasant tank; studying and being studied. The menu changes every day. I was right about evolutionary mayhem, there are so many varieties. My wife has learnt to read their lips and is teaching me. We have a delicate balance to strike, we must be interesting but not too much. I have a rapport with one of the female creatures; she will not let them cut me up just to see how I work.

The trouble is, she cannot control her eggs like my wife did. The planet has a huge moon and it causes an egg to pop out each time it orbits. That was not in my thesis but just adds to the mayhem. I must find a way to stop them being fertilised so that she stays to protect us.

# Dolphins

'Thank you for coming on our sunset trip this evening. This is just a short explanation of what we hope to see. The tour is round a group of islands which were the private residence of the former president. For thirty years no unauthorised boats were allowed near. These were unique circumstances which fostered the marine reserve which has allowed the dolphins to thrive.'

*'Where are we going grandma? Everyone else is going to dinner.' I ask slightly petulantly.*

*'It's our turn tonight. I've been watching you and you are more than ready to take to the stage.' Is her reply and then, 'now where is your mother?'*

To be honest, we will not need to see any dolphins to enjoy this trip. The sea is calm; the sun is glinting on the water and the view as we leave the harbour is sufficient. What would I have thought two thousand years ago to sail into this town, with such an impressive amphitheatre. I expect it felt like paradise back then with abundance on land and sea.

*We are swimming away from the others and I feel in need of entertainment. 'Tell me the story again grandma so that I can pass it on to my own children.'*

*'You've no idea what it feels like to hear you say that. Your mother was never interested.'*

*'I am here you know! And, it was the only story you ever told, but I don't mind listening again if you can't hold it in.' In dolphin speak that phrase is reserved for adults indulging children; encouraging them to exhaust themselves with aquabatics. I can tell that grandma enjoys the compliment of being considered a child and begins her tale.*

*'A hundred generations ago we lived in paradise. The sea was full of fish and you could travel anywhere and be sure of a meal. The only thing you had to do was play – all day. Then the floating islands appeared. The creatures on them are just like us. They can't swim*

very well but they eat fish; they need air to breathe and I have seen a mother feeding her young. They are friendly but mostly they take all the fish.'

'You'll know when we have spotted some dolphins, the captain will change course and then slow down. We think they don't like the noise of the engines. Don't all crowd at the front of the boat; they are just as likely to pop up behind us.'

'The noise started in my great great grandmother's time. It frightens the fish and that is why we are going this way now; so the others can eat in peace. In my mother's time it was really bad. Some of the floating islands exploded and sank; but then it all stopped. The biggest mystery is why the fishing islands were chased away but it recreated paradise; but only here.'

I am first to hear the noise. 'I can hear two, I wonder what they are saying to each other.' Grandma makes a strange sound which I think is the sound of contentment.

'Your mum said exactly the same thing years ago. Off you go, but don't get too close until the noise subsides.' Mum is in the prime of life and can easily outpace either of us, grandma said to her. 'Swim with me, I feel the need of strengthening my memories of life.'

'Up you come! You'll not see anything in this crowd. Look Amy! There are two together. I can't take any pictures holding you so you're going to have to remember this.'

Amy sees her grandma leaving. 'Where are you going grandma?'

'To the back, I can't see anything either.' That is a good decision; they are the only ones there and are rewarded by the appearance of the pair first spotted at the front. Then a smaller dolphin leaps out of the water.

'Look at me,' I squeak.

Grandma sighs, 'I remember when I could do that.' She says to mum. 'You still can, release your inner child and make me feel younger.

The reply is decisive, 'you're not as old as you pretend to be, let's all do it!'

'I think these dolphins are playing hide and seek, what

do you think Amy?' Amy is four years old and does not really know what all the excitement is about. She feels it would be nice to play with the small one who had looked straight at her. They are hiding at the moment but there is a collective 'Oooh' from the group at the front. Three dolphins are porpoising in a most exuberant way in a line between two watching boats. Both captains turn to follow.

*Mum is speeding away and grandma is not far behind. I have a vision of my destiny; one day that will be me. As that thought leaves my mind I hear a loud crash and a scream descending into the water. It is an alien sound but its meaning is clear and I turn for its source. I feel fearless as I approach the floating island and swim between those flailing legs. She is surprisingly light and as we surface her scream turns into a giggle. Her face is close to my air hole so I blast her again. Mum and grandma come close to give me more support.*

'Cut engines.' The boat begins to drift but the dolphins edge closer. The guide, whom you may have thought was only there because of her proficiency in languages, is already in the water with a lifebelt for my precious cargo.

'You see, they are just like us.' Said grandma as we made our way for a well-deserved meal. 'I've seen that woman before and she did not hesitate to save someone else's child.'

I added, 'I don't think she wanted to be rescued, she was enjoying playing.' Mum was not so sure, she had seen most people just standing there holding something, not helping at all.

The enquiry found that the captains of the two boats which collided were negligent but they had acted correctly afterwards. Their (non) punishment was a six month ban from October to March inclusive. The guide would have been famous except she is only recognised when her hair is wet. The dolphins went viral, especially the one which saved the girl. Soft toys exist with a distinctive patch around one eye and there are mermaid dolls suspiciously like Amy. The guide now adds an extra warning, 'do not carry children too close to the sides.'

*I can now keep up with my mum, but only because she is*

*carrying a brother or sister for me. That doesn't mean she can avoid diversion duties. It is now our turn again after the quiet period. We've been told there are now more boats and so the job is even more important. I do my special trick, I've been practicing and can now clear the water and fly. I surface and find myself surrounded by cheering and pointing; those flat sticks are everywhere. I can see the woman who jumped in with the floating ring and she is talking to the people around her. Just think if we could understand each other, her smile is saying something nice.*

'Yes, that is the one who saved the little girl,' and then she thought to herself only, 'and you saved us too.'

## Screen Time

I used to like my job; delivering takeaways to people who were pleased to see you; outside, getting exercise and meeting people. Two years ago I had a lot of regulars on this development. The manor house is still there, the owner must have made a packet selling the land for the houses; no affordable housing here. I could work out who was having a sleepover by where the orders went. One by one the orders stopped, no, moved to the manor. It's not the same, it is a more mundane job; no variety. In fact, the orders are nearly always the same; I never did breakfasts before.

Recently I have been feeling the oddity of it all. I am hardly needed; a robot could do this job. I now only have two deliveries, the manor and the local policeman. His daughter has taken the order once or twice and that is what shocked me into action.

Lunchtime yesterday no-one answered my call at the manor, so I pushed at the door and it was unlocked. It opened onto a gloom; the ghostly faces of children, lit by their screens, were socially distanced in all the ground floor rooms. I went through to the kitchen and placed the order, silently, on the table full of trays.

Another door was open to a workshop beyond. I glanced at a nearby table and froze; starting from my eyes, over my head and down my spine, forking at my legs and finally splaying my toes. Unblinking was the head of the policeman's daughter, her shoulder length hair lay in a neat semi-circle around her on the table. It was almost too realistic, with a calm smile. In the furthest corner was a mannequin dressed in school uniform; they were obviously destined for each other but why.

The flushing of a toilet at the back spurred me to move. I retreated, picked up the delivery and ran outside. I waited for my heart to slow down and then rang the bell. The door opened and a disembodied hand took my bag. That evening I delivered the usual to the policeman and suggested he investigate the manor. I could not tell him why, I just hinted at the strangeness of the orders. He beckoned me in, but I declined, I caught sight of his daughter intent on her screen.

I no longer deliver to the policeman, but his daughter's favourite is now on the manor list; even though I saw her setting off for school when I was delivering breakfast. In fact all the children got to the stop just as the school bus arrived and embarked silently.

I complained that the single large order was too heavy. That was the last time they called on me. I saw my replacement the other day, the way he moves he should be in The Olympics. He does not look like he is enjoying the job, not like I used to.

# The Hunter

When you visit the show caves, do you wonder why you have to pay to see what nature created. You probably accept that some money is needed to maintain the walkways, light the route and generally keep you safe. Some of the exhibits did not grow where you see them. I am a hunter, exploring the depths; looking for interesting formations that can be transported for the ease of your enjoyment. It is only because we light them specially to give form and meaning that they come to life; in our imagination.

When I am hunting I have a special torch; research has shown that the single frequency green light on it does not disturb them. They are not really alive, but if you use a normal light your imagination can play tricks. I often pass uninteresting stalagmites and stalactites in my searches. Who am I to decide; sometimes I return with my eerie green photographs and the artistic director wants to know where one is; so that it can be brought up for illumination.

We used to use technology, to track our route, so that we could find them again. We: yes I was once not the only hunter; my greatest friend, and occasional rival, disappeared ten years ago. He had found something special and returned to get photographs and a precise location. Technology must have failed him because he did not return.

I check my equipment; waterproof boots, hard hat, ball of nylon rope and torches. I tie the rope around a tree and enter. The rope is the method I now use to find my way home from the labyrinth. Sunlight is left behind and my ears become my sight. Drip, drip, drip. Are they warning each other of my approach? Today I can venture further; the rope gets lighter as it unravels my route to safety.

There it is, the Blue Wolf, last seen over ten years ago, by my friend. The shape is unmistakeable and I confirm that it is blue by switching on my main light. It is a malevolent sight;

many shades of blue giving the impression that it is lit from above. It has a full set of white, calcified, teeth and an iron streak of red on its lower jaw. It will not need creative illumination, as I play my light over it, it seems to move; watching me. It is immense; it will frighten the adults, as well as the children.

It was for this that my friend was lost. I try to anchor my rope so that others, more adept at removal than I, can be guided here. I fumble slightly and my light is briefly off. When I find it and re-illuminate this grotto, my blood runs cold. The wolf is no longer there, but behind where it had been is my friend. The thin layer of carbonate which encases him does not hide the terror on his face.

I sweep the light around; the wolf is behind me, blocking my exit. The statue of my friend has a torch and it is angled upwards; the same as mine. Drip, drip, drip; the sound of the water, with its cargo of calcium, landing on my hard hat, is staccato; counting the seconds until I too will become an exhibit, in the Blue Wolf's lair. I switch off my light for one second. It seems to last forever, but I must resist the urge to shorten it. When I flood the scene again the wolf is almost upon me. Keeping the beam trained on my potential nemesis, I can now inch my way around it: and flee.

# Rust

It is all slightly strange so I ask. 'Is this how it all ends? Nothing but water! Just me and you two. I know you think I'm a chatterbox but you have been around forever. Since before the rest of us were born.'

'Be quiet for once. We've never been in this situation before,' says the first of my companions. His friend adds.

'Can you feel the tugging?' There is a murmur of agreement from those close by. 'I think we are being tested just to see how loyal we are to each other.' At least we are still moving; bumping into each other; water on water is soft and soothing. At last we bounced off something different and my companions said simultaneously.

'See we're just contained in something.' I think they are as relieved as I, but still it is very odd.

*'As you can see no current is flowing but if you add a little salt...'*

'Where did they come from? What are you two arguing about?' One of my companions breaks free and leaves us. His friend says.

'He has gone to the dark side. You see that one over there, slightly bigger than you. If he can bond with it they will become powerful destroyers.'

'But it's a trick,' I say, 'look he's being dragged away and I feel hungry.' The food is in the opposite direction. There is a feeding frenzy but I get my share. My companion of many years feels he does not belong here and leaves me. My hunger is sated but I feel exposed. I attach myself to the nearest one like me and we both feel comforted. I introduce myself.

'It's been aeons since I had anyone to have a proper conversation with.'

'Well I'm sure you'll tell me all about it,' is the bored

response.

'As you can see there are bubbles and the current is flowing. If you have brought a bottle, as I suggested, you can capture some and take it home. Do not collect from the cathode it may explode.'

This is a very strange day. First there was only water and now there is only us. Trillion-trillions of us. Obviously it is very noisy and I'm beginning to be glad my new friend is more taciturn. 'What are you hoping for?' I ask.

'To avoid being caught,' is his terse reply.

'But that's our role.' I remonstrate. 'We give life to things.'

'But at what price. I've never been water before and that didn't last long.'

'Oh! That's sad. I've been every kind of water. I was part of a snowflake and then frozen for thousands of years. Deep in the ocean you are squashed so much you can hardly speak. The excitement as you rush to a waterfall never disappoints. To be in a rainforest is tiring but fun. Up every day becoming part of a cloud and then falling down and bouncing off leaves. I've been part of a large hailstone breaking things as we descend too fast to be stopped.' I decide to be less exuberant. 'I heard the cries for help as we filtered through porous rocks. So you want to avoid moving with any crowd not just the wrong crowd.'

'Of course! But think about it, we must be going somewhere special. A whole lot of our kind and nothing else, we must be destined for something.

*'School OK today?'*
*'Yep! I've got something special for Harry's birthday cake.'*
*'Well, you're just in time, what is it?'*
*'Something for the candles.'*

'I think we should make our way to the back of the queue. I don't want to be first for whatever it is.' I agree but we do miss all the fun. The flames were large and most get new partners.

I make an observation. 'You could have been water again, look at all the newlyweds.'

My friend counters. 'Look at the others, they could be with carbon for a very long time. Yes you have a friend to talk to but I was attached so long I ran out of things to say. It's why I'm not very talkative. I expect a few months with you will cure that.'

*'Deep breath Harry!'*

'Oh no! Don't touch anything, we have to get out of here. I was tricked by this millions of years ago.'

*'Hooray! Happy Birthday. I think we need to open a window.'*

'Phew that was close. In and straight out. Now we can escape before anything else sucks us in.'

'I know, let's go join the new water. They'll let us into one of their drops.' I suggest. Floating free with just your comfort buddy is like a holiday from the real business of making things happen. Mixing with water and others like us is safer and you get all the fun of being a raindrop when the time comes.

I learn a lot. 'Why is carbon so grumpy,' I ask.

'It likes to be in a crowd. When it only has us it is reminded of what could have been.'

'Yes I remember I was carbon for a while before I was born when I was lucky to bump into some helium.'

His words of wisdom stuck with me. 'I found that embracing my inner carbon helped me through the static years.' I think my new friend has already found his voice again. He shows it by joining in a chorus of 'Weeeh,' as our raindrop falls and lands on something hard.

'Oi! Don't you know that's dangerous.' An angry voice continues, 'something could get hurt. You all look a bit dazed. Come and join us we could have a party.' I'm not sure what happened next. We were having fun swapping electrons; us, some water and the iron. The sun came out and the water said it was time to go. Here we are three of us tied to two of them.

*'I told you not to worry, it was only a shower. There's just a bit of surface rust. Let's get the concrete on.'*

Suddenly we are surrounded. There is no freedom. The iron does not mind, it is not used to being free. My new friends are sad because they had only been water briefly. My previous friend must have escaped as water. I hope he gets to experience it like I did. I feel I cannot talk about it just now, it would only increase the sadness. I will have to embrace my inner carbon.

# Season Ticket

August first home match

'Na then, thi can't keep thee away then, didst av a good summer?'

'It were all r8, but A miss Satday afternoon.'

'What dust think about all t' changes?'

'Thiv all gone, them as mek a difference.'

'Aye, but next May can't be as bad as last May.'

'Am lookin forrerd to this season. We ad a good run int Premier League but it's not nice allus getting beat and frettin about evry result.'

'So thas banna relax and enjoy it.'

Part way through the match

'Thas not relaxing, is thee?'

'How can A. Thell be trouble, all this passin it back. T'other side 'll pounce when they're laikin about.'

'It's new style. Stop shuttin thee eyes, thal miss arft game.'

'They're not a team to watch if thas of a nervous disposition, are thi'

The end of the match

'We w winning, ow can they snatch defeat fromt jaws o victory?'

'Be fair, it were a draw, but thid better not do it too offen.'

'It's gunner be a long season, no mistake. I might gi my ticket to someone who needs therapy fer bein too optimistic.'

April

'Promoted already, it's been a joy comin ere this season.'

'Tha ners, Av learnt not to worry. Th'opposition as to get at least two in afore th'old me comes out.'

'Av noticed, tha stopped frettin when we scored twice in added time genst Rotherham to win 3-2.'

'Since then Am a changed man, what'st worst that can appen now? Can't see it mi sen.'

October

'Dusta remember last year?'

'It's only thing keeping me coming, wiv lost all four this season at home, trounced.'

'We av a good goalie!'

'That only meks it worse.'

'T'manager's still upbeat.'

'Tha siz, A knew someone needed therapy fer bein too optimistic.'

# Jemimah's Choice

I have to be honest, it has not been as I expected. Yes, the facility is only accessible from the sea but there is no overt security. In fact everyone has been very open with me. Not one sign 'no admittance' or 'authorised personnel only'. I suppose it feels like home when not even the toilets give you a clue as to what may surprise you when you blunder in. The site has a group of workers who are loosely families. I have been here to teach their children.

My pupils are all roughly the same age. It brings to mind those deep space missions where young couples blast off to colonise another planet and celebrate when they arrive. Except the fathers are all in their forties and their partners are mixed ages. The children have been candid; is that another quirk of their upbringing? For their fathers this has been a second chance after failed relationships. I have tried to imagine how they persuaded their new loves into this situation.

'Let's go to the Caribbean on holiday forever!' Would have excited me but making a baby would have been a bit of a downer. In the seventies the site was a peace and love commune and there is a thread in the current occupants attached to that ideal. There is a huge fuel tank and they are proud that it is hardly needed. They take sustainability seriously. 'You will wonder why you needed air-conditioning in a few weeks.' I was told when I arrived. They make their own natural insect repellent which you have to wear because it repels humans who do not have it.

I was given a tour by the head of the facility when I arrived. A lot of effort was going into producing very little; I was shown a dripping tap. 'That is what we make. Only one ton a year. Not enough to sell it. We have proved it works but now need to find a way to scale up.'

'If it is the elixir of life that is enough to make a fortune.' I said this to show I was a primary school teacher not a spy. His reply then has meaning now.

'I will remember that when we market it, we need enough for many lives.' The conclusion of the tour was most welcome. Over a low ridge there is a safe pool; safe in the sense that there is nothing to bite you; as long as you smear their repellent goo on yourself. He took his clothes off and dived in and bid me do the same. After a few minutes of exhilarating cooling we swam to a particular corner.

'This is where the smooth rocks are, we can sit here modestly.' I believe formal meetings are sometimes held in saunas in Finland. This was an equivalent. 'Although we recruited you for your teaching abilities, we want you to be an observer. The children have had an idyllic upbringing so far. They know about the outside world but only in video. We need to know what difficulties they will face when we close down and they scatter across the planet.'

That was a strange choice of words, after all, they are not an alien invasion force. 'Surely you know what the world is like.' I realised this was a silly thing to say so I continued. 'I suppose you have forgotten. It took me by surprise when you stripped off. Would I have been sacked if I hadn't done the same.'

'No, we chose you from many candidates, but it helps that you are already assimilated.' The 'getting to know my class' was completed five minutes later. They arrived, led by an older boy, and all joined us in the pool. My tour guide left, his nakedness completely ignored as he got out and put on his clothes without drying.

There was little point being introduced to them all. They were more interested in playing and I would not recognise them with clothes and dry hair. I sought out the teenage boy who had led them here. 'Are you my teaching assistant?' I think he liked the idea.

'No, I'm just a few years older than them. My mum is the chief scientist. I've been here longer than the others. My name is James by the way.' My first impression was that he was too nice to survive in the real world. Whilst I was thinking this he added enigmatically, 'I am the reason all of this is here.'

I decided not to ask for an explanation, maybe I should have. 'Am I responsible for them all now?'

'No, they expect you to leave. I'll be staying until the last one gets out.'

That was my introduction to my situation. I had seen the head of the facility put his clothes in the water when he left. I did likewise and had the joy of feeling I was still in the water all the way back. The children all had learning programmes. My job simply seemed to be listening to them explaining what they were doing.

If I were a real teacher I would think this was all very strange but I am a secret agent in receive mode, looking for secrets. James keeps me informed. All his life his mother has talked to him about her work, not technically, but as a form of release. He told me that when he was only five years old and the other children were newborn she had told him.

'They are here because of what we learnt from you.' Later when he asked why there were no more she had said. 'Because we can choose when to have them.' He had found out that they lived in the tropics because what they made needed to stay warm. I had been given a narrative when I was assigned to this job.

'From intercepts we think they are developing an oral version of their contraceptive injection. We think it will be sold as a weapon to the highest bidder. They have been acquiring bottling plants all over the world.'

Everything I learn can be bent to this story. James is genetically special in some way. They have contraception they can rely on. They have a problem keeping their substance active and they need more. The head of facility had talked about closing down as if these problems may be solved. I have one other observation. They are not fanatics but they worry about climate change and think there are too many people in the world. This is apparent from the learning programmes and simply the way the children talk. If it is wisdom then it has been received.

A special day has arrived. James' mother makes the announcement. 'Who would like to go on holiday?' The assembled crowd are aware of what has been achieved. 'Yes, we've finally done it. You are the pioneers who have proved it works and now we can now make enough. We don't need to hide any longer.' There is self-congratulatory murmur. 'We thought you would all like to go on a cruise, somewhere cool.'

That is almost the end of my job. I relay the news to my handler. 'Hi mum! I'll be home soon. They're moving everything from here and the children will all be away from here on holiday.' They had chosen a plausible looking woman to be my mother. 'Do you have dates, I'm trying to organise something for grandma's birthday.' This is code for an assault.

'They'll be gone in a week, but I think I'm staying a bit longer.'

'That's a shame, well maybe we can contact you to join in; a week on Sunday.' The assumption is that all my external communication is monitored so we still use these role playing methods. I am not sure they fool anyone.

The day has arrived. I wish I could tell them not to come. The only thing which has been removed is most of the people. James, her mother and a handful of non-technical staff remain. I decide to stick to the plan. Originally I was meant to keep the children safe now I only have one to look after. I suggest a swim and a picnic. He looks at me trying to answer the question 'why' without actually asking it. Finally he agrees.

'Mum told me to always do what you ask, however strange.' Like a good son he tells her what is happening whilst I assemble our favourite snacks. This involves a walk to the food store which is situated away from the main area. I marvel at how well-stocked it is, perhaps everyone will return after the holiday. I have learnt to scan anything that I take so that the inventory is up to date.

The residential part of the site is like any other resort with individual lodges for guests. Each building has its own solar panels and batteries so that it is independent of whatever happens elsewhere. The whole effect is of a holiday destination for those who want to be close to nature.

It is not far to the pool but the effort is always such that you are desperate to immerse yourself. It is the silkiness of its cool caress which banishes most thoughts. I must tell James that it is normal for boys his age to wear something when swimming. When we emerge refreshed we waste no time in covering up. Our goo impregnated clothes are an important protection and we quickly administer facials to ourselves.

We are silently eating when there are sounds from the beach. Unmistakeably powerful boats have arrived and disgorge men and machines bent on destruction. I do not immediately react as you would expect and he says, 'you were expecting them, weren't you?' I am lost for words and it could be the end of our friendship but his tone is not combative. 'What are they going to do?' Before I can answer a small explosion is absorbed by the forest.

'If I tell you to stay here, will you do it?'

'No.'

'Well stay close and do what I do. To answer your question, I thought I knew what they were going to do, but that explosion was not them.'

As we approached the ridge I rub soil on my face and creep to the top. James is beside me, no longer a boy, invisible except for his wide, white eyes. Soldiers are prowling uncertainly; a hail of bullets causes a beautiful bird to fall from a tree. There is a sequence of choreographed explosion. The walls of the canteen block blow outwards and the roof descends to thunderous applause.

In the silence which follows I hear one side of a communication. 'It's a trap, there is no-one here.' They retreat to where they landed and prepare to destroy as much as they can. We are in the firing line if any of their projectiles overshoot so I motion to James that we should leave.

'Stay!' A voice commands. 'You'll miss the main event.' James' mother is stood a little way down the slope. She looks at her tablet and taps. A display worthy of bonfire night begins. All the buildings collapse as small detonations weaken them. The finale involves the unused reserve fuel tank which floods the area. The ignition is not explosive, like a mythical creature tentacles of flame move outwards before joining to become an all-consuming fire. The soldiers leave, no doubt to be congratulated on a successful mission.

I know that I am about to be taunted. When I turn away from the climactic moment I see she has been patiently waiting. The men, who presumably set the explosives, have already left. 'Don't worry Ms Bond, you are a woman it is no longer your problem. Would you like to remain ignorant of what you have just witnessed?'

'If the truth helps me survive, I'll take it.'

'Good! But it may change how you survive. You're aware of our business and through the communication trail which we let you find you think we are up to no good. Our male contraceptive injection has been a great success. It is just a pity that it is permanent so, mainly, only men who want no more children take it up. There are millions but if we could reverse it there are billions.'

'That seems an admirable aspiration.' I say, there is a whole chapter in the training manual on flattery. I remember I had been told they were working on a soluble version of their jab which could be used as a weapon. Armies are filled with young men for whom infertility is the worst form of disability. To show I was aware of what we thought was happening I added. 'So you're not going to hold all the men in the world to ransom?'

'If it were that easy, eh? It is already happening. A side effect of our injection is that there is a waterborne version already. Every time one of our customers has a pee some escapes into the environment. It seems to be indestructible. We discovered it when a man attended an infertility clinic and he had our product in him. That was about the time James was born. Sorry James I'm not your mother, if it's any consolation I wish I was.'

I look at James, he seems to be taking the news very calmly. I wonder if he suspected already. She continues, 'your father was immune to the jab, as are you. He, and your real mother's, view was that it was our fault and therefore responsibility.' She is a bit disappointed that we have no comments; playing to a small audience can be dispiriting.

'Actually it was our fault, we knew about one in a thousand were immune. A laboratory mix up on test samples was the real problem. So, all these years we've been working on an antidote using James' DNA as a clue. We came here for many reasons. Top of the list was not wanting to have any more environmental escapes. James is lovely but we didn't want any more. It was quickly obvious the process would have to be warm so why waste energy in a northern latitude. Finally we had to test it, I had sleepless nights woken by nightmares of deformed babies.'

Everything I had seen had a reason but I wondered about the apparent secrecy. 'How many accidentally infertile men do you know about? Why didn't you just own up?' I ask naively. Her response lets me know what she thinks of my question.

'Everyone of those affected would want compensation. A thousand times as many men would want a free test. We would be bankrupt and not able to research. You spies live in a simple world of good and bad.'

'So why did you get us involved?'

'How would you have told the world? Sorry, we caused a problem but we've got a solution and you're not going to like it. We needed to get the attention of governments without it becoming common knowledge.'

'It's not going to affect many people is it?' I asked, obviously a long way from understanding the power being unleashed.

'The genie said you have three wishes, use them wisely. Our first wish was for a male contraceptive which could easily be checked for. Our second wish was a way to turn it on or off so that every child is wanted. Our third wish was for the whole world to have access so that it could not be used as a weapon. We have started on the third wish.'

'What have we just destroyed?' I do not really need to ask.

'The antidote. The second wish. Not enough for everyone. We could have sold it for a lot of money but would probably have given it away. Your friends chose to arrive with guns.'

'Was there an alternative? You convinced us all of your bad intent.'

She crushed me with her reply. 'You were the alternative. Don't you think it strange that you could subvert our recruitment process so easily.'

In the exchange with my handler when I was given the date, via 'grandma's birthday', I had wanted to say, 'wait you've got it all wrong,' but could not think of a reason why. I was supposed to become an intermediary, explaining, almost an interpreter of two different world views.

'So it's my fault the world will come to an end.'

'It is the fault of the world; they trained you to look for evil. Our chosen course will save many first world governments an agonising choice. They would have been the ones with endemic infertility. They would probably have levelled the playing field, in the same way' This is a very cynical view of the effects of technology in the hands of non-scientists. Her last words on the subject remove any idea that I really understand what is happening. 'You still have a choice.'

James spoke. 'It's not the end of the world is it? It will be my world won't it?' She tosses a memory stick towards me.

'Keep James alive and with that you will be able to recreate what we have just destroyed.' Then to James she said. 'You are correct that it could be your world; except you will not be in control of your body. I think I have been a good stepmother and taught you well. Use your knowledge to keep Ms Bond alive so that she can make her choice. Don't think about following me.'

I know I will have to think before acting on the events of the day. When she has disappeared from view, I turn to James and say, 'what would you like for tea?'

'I'll go cut a pineapple, beans on beans would be nice.' He replies. We amble past the ruins of an alternative world. I head for the food store and he for the farm. We meet half an hour later in the kitchen of my lodge. Being normal allows one to think. There is no rush, we could survive here for months if necessary. All the computer resources are ash, co-locating them had fostered community.

'Do you know how to bake bread?' I ask savouring my last crumb of toast.

'I would if we still had the internet.'

'If we had that they would know we were still here and come for us. How long do you think we can stay here do you think?'

James is unnervingly calm. 'I have grown up on tinned food, I expect you would break first! Anyway the food stock computer will have the answer.'

He does not realise what he has just said but he likes my grin. 'We're in this together; I need you; that is a brilliant idea.' I spend the next two weeks on the computer with the memory stick. I do not understand most of it but there is a journal kept by James' stepmother. This contains her thoughts. James gets a lot of praise. *He is so well-adjusted. I wonder if the genetic difference which makes him immune also affects his personality.*

It is the last day of my perusal and I am almost up to date. *Jemimah is a disappointment. She is not asking any questions so I fear the conclusion will be what I suspected all along. I will have to tell James he is adopted. I think he already knows; he has been behaving differently since Ms Bond arrived and it is not just puberty.*

In one paragraph I go from naughty schoolgirl to Femme Fatale. I need to know that I am neither. James has made tinner, tinned dinner, he is right that he will survive longer than I. I make the observation and he amazes me yet again.

'I've been around all the lodges and found a lot of money; dollars and local. There is a path up the cliff at the back and then it's not far to the town.'

'You mean we can have bread!'

'With a bit of effort, when you've finished in your cave. What did you learn today?'

Each day I have told him what I have discovered so any reticence now would be obvious. 'First I was a disappointment and you suspected you were adopted after my arrival.' He has such a beautiful blush.

'You were the first woman I noticed, actually the only one so far. I can be very observant.' He blushed again. 'Your stomach is flat, unlike all the other women, mothers, except mine.' I suddenly feel responsible for completing his education.

'Tomorrow you can show me the path; we will go and buy some bread and then observe every type of woman.'

The very last comment in the journal is – *if you show this information to someone who understands it you could be in production in about a year; plus however long it takes to get them on board.*

Most days we visit the town but every day I envisage a different scenario of how I might save the world. They usually end badly. I now understand the plan where I would have discovered everything and explained it whilst someone was willing to listen to me. Now my crimes are compounded by my silence.

After six months news filters through about a fertility pandemic. The biggest shock is when the woman serving in the bakers says, 'watch out for your son. Some of the tourists are here for a seed. The islands haven't been affected yet and boys are a better bet anyway.' I look in the mirror at home and notice her bread and cakes have made my stomach slightly rounded.

When I tell James he comforts me, 'don't worry I think of you as an older sister.'

The next time I am in the bakery I surprise the woman by only buying bread and entering into more conversation than normal. 'James is not my son but I am responsible for him. I've known him all his life. He is the nicest boy I've ever known and what you said last time worried me. He needs a normal experience with a girl not a desperate woman.' My voice is getting quieter as I talk and she replies with a whisper.

'My daughter is slightly older and already fending off the boys. If the disease arrives here she will have no excuse.' At normal volume she adds. 'You can always send your son to collect the order if you can't make it.' I can see the disease in the chilled drinks cabinet which is an essential on a tourist island in this climate.

I expect you are disappointed in me; taking no action; making no decision; an actionless woman. If you are reading this you will be living in the world I chose. I hope you like it. At this moment, six months after being given the task, I still have no definite ideas on what different futures will be like. The world is not waiting for my decision.

I will set out my defence. When I discovered I was a "disappointment" I thought 'what do you expect.' Spies discover secrets, there were none; it was all open. It looked just like I was led to believe. Afterwards no-one came to look for me or even to see what had been destroyed. The first weeks I was discovering the truth but then what? The cynical comment that with the knowledge of what is happening "my government would choose to level the playing field" – haunts me. Would I be welcome?

During this time there is one more thing which stops me from doing anything. James is too young to become a laboratory specimen. In my world he would be a secret. When he was a baby being special did not affect him but now it would be the end of his self. There will be more men like him who could be used but even that would be a secret.

The following week James comes home with five loaves, three buns and the love of his life. The latter is so obvious it is embarrassing. I spend my days helping in the bakery, after all the daughter is otherwise engaged. I know their love nest is not their eventual future but it is a privilege to watch its development. Another three months pass and I meet my first desperate woman.

The bakery has a few tables for those who like their cake

on a plate. It is the way she asks for a shot of rum with her coffee that alerts me. I help myself to some rum and go to talk. 'I didn't realise I had a twin sister.' Not a bad opener since there was a passing resemblance.

'Except I don't have your "I belong here" tan.' Is her friendly reply.

'It only takes a year or so, if you stick around,' and then I whisper, 'it is all over, we are quite laid back here.' She is in need of someone to unload to. I clink my glass with hers. 'Here's to paradise.'

'Not if you came here for a baby.'

'I'm sure there are lots of men willing.'

'But they are not willing to take the test.' This is new to me and my puzzled look elicits the following. 'I brought a stock of those tablets.' My expression does not change. 'Where have you been? That woman who worked for the vasectomy jab company is our saviour. I know they had to do something sharpish because they lost all their customers. To be able to judge a man's fertility with a tablet in his pee is genius.'

I am more surprised than she expects which helps us bond more, 'and you haven't found a man yet?'

'They don't want to know.'

'At least they are honest, they can't lie if they don't know the truth.' This is my defence of men who may suddenly lose their raison d'etre.

'I booked a two week holiday and the first week has been a waste of time.' I fall silent for long enough to intrigue her. 'What?' Is all she asks.

'I'm protecting someone, come back at closing time if you are interested.' Obviously she is! As we scramble down the cliff path I begin to explain. 'He will not need a test although I expect he will be amused to try. I'm protecting him because he is an innocent. He has proved himself and is more than in love. He does not know you are coming.'

I think I have said enough to reduce expectations and impress that she has great responsibility. James understands why she is here. Over tinner his new love asks.

'Why would you want to bring a child into this world?' A strange question from one who is doing just that. Of course, she will understand the answer better than anyone. The answer, when it comes, is perfect.

'When I arrived I was only interested in not being the last of my line. We have a picture, when I was young, of four generations of women. I have this yearning for a daughter. After a week of false starts I realise I need far more. I already have a 'dad' waiting at home to welcome whatever I create; but you would be an auntie.'

Later we mull over the evening. 'I will make myself scarce when James comes round.'

'You seem sure he will.'

'You said everything that was needed, but it does mean you can't go home. You will have to stick around to be an auntie too.'

She sighs. 'This is far more difficult than I imagined; more than a simple transaction. There is nothing left at home. Do you want to know the greatest irony; we run a shop for baby clothes and equipment. It wouldn't be fair to call my husband and say I'm not coming home.'

My mind is racing through the future. The tableaux of the evening shows that the new world order could work; it relies a lot on empathy. Our idyll is not the world; I need to return to the hustle and bustle to understand what is actually happening. If I travel as myself I will be picked up at the border.

'I can tell him.' I say as a plan is forming. 'I can leave now you are here.' She may be feeling tricked into coming with me; what will she make of my next suggestion. 'I will use your ticket and explain everything to him. I just need to change my hair colour to match yours.'

'No you don't.' She is obviously going to reject my idea and I am about to try again when she adds. 'This isn't my hair colour. I thought by looking different I could be different and go through with the plan.'

'I will enjoy meeting your husband, he must be exceptionally understanding.'

We have a lot of fun planning what I will do in arrivals. A few days later I am failing to get through the e-passport gates and therefore showing someone else's picture to a bored border official. Maybe she is the boredest and I am through - to surprise a man who is expecting his wife. He is staring past me as I kiss him full on the lips. 'You didn't recognise me did you? Take me home for a proper bath.'

I set off so that he is looking at my rear view; in one of the few dresses he will recognise; dragging a wonky case which is definitely theirs. We are in the short stay car park before he asks, 'who are you?'

'Your wife has to stay longer, so I'm the replacement. Let's get in the car, I'm freezing.' I have to explain everything before he is willing to set off. As we leave he observes.

'My real wife would have insisted we leave to reduce the parking charge. I think we are going to get on.' We do become good friends especially after I agree to play a joke on her by pretending he was not there to meet me. He does not realise he is emigrating when he books a flight to be reunited with her. Before he goes I decide to test reactions to ideas.

'If I told you I could prove that all the problems you are having have been created deliberately, what would you say?' I said this a propos of nothing and he studied me before replying.

'Anyone else and I would say, "you and a million others." If I knew something I would keep it to myself, unless you want to be infamous.' His look says that he believes me so I ask another question.

'Are you happy with how things are turning out?'

'We left it late to start a family. Our attempts were not going well. This could be a better outcome for us.'

'So you would say you are a winner.'

'That's not the way to look at it. Ten years ago I didn't know how desperate we would become. Back then if we had been told it would never happen we would have adjusted. To be a winner or loser you have to be in the race.'

'I think I'm jealous, I've never been interested in that particular race until now.' I have no idea how he interpreted that comment but I think it went deep into his list of things to feel good about. It showed in his expression; it was James' stepmother who introduced me to the concept. All the men who were immune to the jab displayed a Mona Lisa smile when they were told, because they were special. It extended to James' father who could not be angry about the mix up that had resulted in James.

I spend my days in their shop, there are very few customers. It is now two years since it all started. In the public domain there are shrill voices advocating every kind of opposing action. In private there is sadness which sometimes comes in through the door of the shop. After the first one I keep a stock of holiday brochures to make recommendations. James is a father many times over but a dad only once, so far.

I made my choice, months ago. The truth must never be known about the cause; the world cannot cope with such self-knowledge. Do we need a cure? It would take a long time to 'accidentally' stumble on the process. I know that many are trying. There is news every few weeks of a breakthrough but people are becoming less interested.

I am trying to imagine the future when it comes in one day, cautiously. I am taking down the Closing Down banners. When they are stashed away you would not know. The shop is still full. Everything Must Go has never been so ignored.

'I was wondering if I could buy a few things.' He asks this as if we are dealing in illicit goods. At the beginning some customers were followed, it is an obvious declaration to be seen leaving the shop with something 0-3 months. I turn the door sign to Closed.

'Too late, you'll have to steal it now.' He looks slightly distressed, perhaps my delivery is a bit too sharp. He seems to recover when I smile.

'Maybe you could help me decide what to steal. My

daughter-in-law is expecting twins, due soon, a boy and a girl.' Slack-jawed is a state of mind and I was exhibiting it. 'I know it's amazing but that's only the start of it. They've gone into hiding. First to avoid seductive women and then their angry husbands.'

I decide one truth needs to be known. 'I have a statistic. Only about one in one thousand are blessed like your son so your daughter-in-law will have to come to terms with sharing him. Maybe the twins will help.' I'm glad he sees my last comment as amusing because I have more information.

'It is not common knowledge, yet, but his son may be similarly blessed so he will have to be a good role model. He is a son himself so what do you think that means?' In a cashless society how does the penny drop. It is his turn to be slack-jawed. 'I think you should take a test.' I suggest.

'Even if I were no-one would want me.' It is then that I see the future. He may be old but he is genetically a good bet; probably ten years older than he looks. I implant a thought.

'Take the test tonight. A discerning woman would select you and her husband would not feel threatened. Come round tomorrow, park at the back and you can have everything in the shop; I hope your house is big enough. I expect you will need it all in the end.'

It takes all day; several carloads. Luckily he does have a big house with a drive so our comings and goings are not noticed. He had the Mona Lisa smile so I knew the result of the test. My situation is precarious. I am still incognito having not revealed my presence to my, former, employers. I am helping to sell the house so the funds can go to Jameswick, not a bad name. I get an offer I cannot refuse.

He does not seem to be tired by all the work today. In fact he seems slightly younger in well-worn clothes. Never judge a sperm by its cover. He sits across the kitchen table from me summoning courage to ask. 'Are you a discerning woman? I feel a little out of practice and I want to be a good role model.'

## About The Author

Angela/654321/1234 – a biography

I was born in Salisbury in 2153. I have written many plays for the radio often on themes which address contemporary problems. That makes me a nudger but of course in my time that is a secret. This collection of short stories has been selected by volunteers at the National Archive, where many more flights of fancy can be found.

Printed in Great Britain
by Amazon